HIGH & DRY

AMULET BOOKS
NEW YORK

HIGH
&DRY

A NOVEL

SARAH SKILTON

Library of Congress Cataloging-in-Publication Data

Skilton, Sarah.

High and dry / by Sarah Skilton.

pages cm

Summary: Framed for a stranger's near-fatal overdose at a party, blackmailed into finding a mysterious flash drive everyone in school seems anxious to suppress, and pressured by his shady best friend to throw an upcoming game, high school soccer player Charlie Dixon spends a frantic week trying to clear his name, win back the girl of his dreams, and escape a past that may be responsible for all his current problems.

ISBN 978-1-4197-0929-6

[1. Mystery and detective stories. 2. Mojave Desert—Fiction. 3. California—Fiction.] I. Title.

PZ7.S6267Hi 2014

[Fic]—dc23

2013025535

Printed and bound in U.S.A.

10 9 8 7 6 5 4 3 2 1

Amulet Books are available at special discounts when purchased in quantity for premiums and promotions as well as fundraising or educational use. Special editions can also be created to specification. For details, contact specialsales@abramsbooks.com or the address below.

115 West 18th Street

New York, NY 10011

www.abramsbooks.com

FOR JOE AND ELLIOT

THE EX BEFORE THE EX

I WASN'T INVITED, BUT I SHOWED UP TO THE PARTY ANYWAY so I could talk to Ellie Chen and find out why she dumped me two weeks ago. It was a choir party at Maria Posey's place, in celebration for killing it at the state qualifier yesterday, so I figured Ellie and her songbird friends would be there.

I didn't figure they'd be mixing it up with my new crowd from soccer and my old crowd from, well, whatever it is Ryder does these days.

I parked a few blocks away and walked up the hill, shivering. It might've been cold outside, and it might not have been. I couldn't tell anymore. Palm Valley, California, is just another place that disregards the seasons. It was January, but that didn't mean anything.

I was only cold because I remembered what it was like to be warm; the year I'd spent with Ellie was the warmest of my life.

When she moved here from New York, I could tell right away she was different. She was smart in a way that didn't make you feel stupid, and beautiful in a way that didn't make you feel ugly. It was like by having those things, and being that way, she made everyone around her believe they were more and better, too.

Now I drank to keep warm.

For Christmas, Granddad had given me his antique flask. The real present was inside, refillable every time I visited him at the hospital. He didn't need to bribe me with booze, though. I liked the old guy and I would've shown up every week no matter what. I liked his vintage magazines and I liked sitting and talking with him at Lancaster Medical while he recovered from pneumonia. Sometimes we'd just play cards and let the hours pass. Unlike my parents, he talked *to* me instead of over me.

The conversations I had with my parents didn't seem to require my presence.

Outside Maria Posey's million-dollar tract home on Western Avenue, I toasted Granddad and sipped my Christmas gift, wincing at the taste. The San Gabriel Mountains were oppressive dark outlines against a gray, smog-choked sky. They practically disappeared on nights like this, but I could still feel them there, separating me from Los Angeles and Pasadena and all the other places that might've been worth living in.

I'd just stumbled through Maria's doorway when my first ex, the ex before Ellie, slithered toward me out of nowhere and looped her arm around mine.

"It's been a month, Dix. You gotta let it go," Bridget said.

"Two weeks and four days," I corrected her, scanning the crowded living room for Ellie. The air was charged, and a few sets of eyes found mine and squinted in curiosity or disapproval. It was hard to tell which.

"It's not that kind of party," Bridget said, wrapping her fingers around my flask and lowering it out of sight between our bodies.

"It is for me," I said.

The hallway and kitchen were packed, too, and I considered mosh-pitting my way through, but Bridget tightened her noose of an arm around mine.

"Don't make a scene. Hang out with me instead," she said. Her large green eyes were like emerald caves, so huge a guy could stroll right into them and stay forever if he didn't mind giving up his own mind. According to Ellie, emeralds had a tranquilizing effect. Screw the Ramones—I didn't want to be sedated.

Bridget leaned against me and I glanced down to where her curves seemed to be inviting my hands on a date. I kept my expression neutral and forced my gaze back up to her lips, which were full and dark and red. Her strawberry blonde hair fell in loose curls over her shoulders, and she smelled like a dream, lush and harmless, but I knew better.

Whoever coined the phrase "girl next door," intending it to mean sweet or innocent, never met Bridget. We used to be tight, but she hadn't given me the time of day in years. Her sudden affection made me suspicious. Just like her emerald eyes, it was too good to be true. You can always spot a fake because it has no imperfections.

I shook her loose and staggered through the living room, dodging couples perched on couches or sprawled on the floor. The room swayed, like the house had become unmoored. I half expected to look out the window and discover a black ocean because we'd all been transported to Semester at Sea. But the floor moved only for me.

Everybody was talking about college admissions, scholarships, essays, and financial aid. Maybe that's why I hadn't been invited: my future was set, while theirs were still in flux.

I fought for balance and caught snippets of deadline-this and deadline-that, all while scanning, scanning, scanning for Ellie.

A couple of my soccer teammates (Patrick and Josh) gave me the nod, or maybe they were indicating heads-up, because suddenly Maria Posey, hostess and head songbird, stepped into my path and scowled.

"Why are *you* here, *Charlie Dixon?*" She threw her words like darts, apparently believing people's names could be used as insults. Or maybe just mine could.

"The beckhams are here, Ellie's here. I'm the epicenter of that Venn diagram," I slurred, and poked her on the shoulder to make my point.

She was disgusted, either by my breath or by the fact that I'd brought math to the party.

"Are you drunk?" she demanded. "I don't want you vomming all over my parents' carpet."

I didn't dignify that with a response. "I just want to say hi to Ellie, okay?"

With a last name like Posey, the pressure was on, but as always, Maria met the challenge. She struck a good one: hip cocked, hand out, eyebrow raised. It was quite a balancing act. I wondered if she'd practiced it in front of the mirror before guests arrived. The Velvet Rope, she could call it.

"Invite?" she demanded again.

"Must've gotten caught in my spam folder."

"Spam folders don't spontaneously generate invites. You didn't make the cut."

"Ellie's here, so I can be here," I pointed out.

"She broke up with you last year."

"Last year was a few days ago!" I took a deep breath. "Two seconds, okay? Then I'll leave."

Her eyes narrowed. "Fine. At least serve a purpose and sign my petition while you're here."

"What's it for? To ship you off to Vassar early or something?"

"It's to convince Principal Jeffries to let the girls' choir perform at graduation."

Ah, graduation: the collective obsession of my classmates—save for me, of course. When you know exactly where you're going, the future holds little charm.

Maria handed me a stack of papers, and I indicated for her to turn around so I could sign it against her back.

When that was through, I found myself alone in the kitchen, turning in a circle, debating which exit was most likely to lead me to Ellie. Should I go back and retrace my steps? Or forge ahead in a new direction?

A Hispanic girl passed through on her way to the living room, her long, dark hair almost obscuring her large, hollow eyes. She looked like a sad girl in search of a tragedy. I could steer her toward mine, but it would cost her a finder's fee.

The sad girl and I glanced at each other. I didn't recognize her and we hadn't been introduced, so I didn't say a word. Every year it gets harder and harder to tell freshmen and sophomores from upperclassmen, and it's not worth the risk engaging them to find out.

I watched her leave, then spun some more—retrace steps, or forge new path?—until someone called my name. My oldest friend, Ryder.

"Hey," he said. An unlit cigarette dangled from his mouth, and he fiddled with a box of orange Tic Tacs, rolling it up and down his knuckles like it was a coin and he was a bored magician. "Didn't expect to see you here."

He was more out of place at this party than I was, and we both knew it. "Ditto," I said.

His dark hair was just long enough to tuck behind his ears, and it stuck out a little from under the ratty, knitted black cap he always wore. His eyes were bloodshot, his nose a little red, and his T-shirt had holes in it, but he still looked like a jock—albeit a jock who'd accidentally dressed himself as a stoner.

He shrugged. "I'm a sucker for songbirds. I'm sure you can relate. Gonna win the game on Friday? Agua Dulce." He drew the "l" out like taffy.

"That's the plan."

He didn't say anything else right away; just looked at me with an expression I couldn't read, empty as an ashtray in a house of former nic addicts.

"I'm heading out, but let's grab lunch on Tuesday. Off-campus? Find me if I don't find you." Ryder walked out the front door before I could answer.

I nodded anyway, and the floor lurched sideways as I wobbled toward the balcony.

Ryder had two inches and thirty pounds on me and he could've played varsity in just about any sport, but he'd failed the drug test freshman year, and failed to care all the years after that. When I met him the summer before sixth grade, he'd been all-American wholesome in his Little League baseball uniform, a star with limitless choices, limitless directions.

As if in deference to his former capacity for greatness, the party had rearranged itself to let him pass, so the direction he'd come from was now an open path for me, too, straight out to the balcony.

I tipped my flask to lap up fresh courage, and when I lowered it, there she was, standing outside in the windy January air, her back to me, in a face-off with the moon over who was more fickle.

A guy stood next to her, leaning against the railing, speaking intimately in her ear. The balcony wrapped around the side of the house, giving them plenty of room, so why were they standing so close together, arms touching?

"Ellie," I shouted.

The guy jumped and stepped aside: Fred from English class, looking frail and pasty like a good debate team nerd should.

Ellie turned around and stared at me. I stared back, dehydrated and dizzy. Her skin was smooth and pale. It reminded me of a cup of milk slowly being poured right before someone yanks the glass away. I was so thirsty, and she was just out of reach.

Her hands were small and tense at her sides, like doves waiting to be released into the air. Her silky black hair was pulled into a loose bun, held together by a lacquered stick with gold Chinese characters painted on it. A few loose strands framed her forehead. She wore a little bit of eye makeup, just enough to prove she didn't need any. This was the "Natural Look" magazines always advise women to go for but no girl can actually pull off. Unless they're Ellie.

I wanted to cup her face in my hands and give her a kiss hello. Her lips were wonderfully soft looking; they never left a mark on my face, almost as if she'd never been there at all, and now I realized I wished she had. Worn lipstick. Left behind some evidence that she and I had really happened.

"What are you doing here, Charlie?" Her voice was soft and low and disappointed, so soft I had to lean in to hear.

"Your brother told me where I could find you."

A smile tugged at one corner of her lips. "He always liked you."

"Funny thing," I said. "You used to like me, too."

"I still do," she said, sounding hurt.

"Can I talk to you for a second?"

"About what?" She backed up and knocked into the railing. I covered the distance between us, but not too close, never too close.

I'd waited a year to ask her out, and on our first date I knew she was too good for me, but I pretended I didn't know, and I spent the next eight months waiting for her to come around to it, too.

Two weeks and four days ago I had agreed to meet her at Café Kismet for a cup of coffee. I came with a basket of pomegranates, her favorite, picked fresh from the tree in Granddad's backyard.

She showed up with a tired, regretful expression and broke it to me gently. But she never told me why.

I sat there long after she left, till closing time, unable to move. There were plastic Christmas lights hanging all over Rancho Vista Boulevard, mocking me with their cheer while my coffee turned cold, then bitter. When I got kicked out of the café, I walked around for hours without going anywhere, just so I wouldn't have to go home. I walked until the lights spun and blurred and flickered in my wet gaze like real candles. I walked until every single one gave up and blinked off, gone as if the desert wind had blown them out.

I could think of a million reasons for her to ditch me, but I didn't know *her* reason.

"You said hi. Now you need to leave," said Maria, tugging on my arm. She'd been head songbird since sophomore year, no small feat, and she ruled the other girls with an iron fist. Most of the time. Rumor had it there'd been a power play at the state qualifier in Pomona yesterday, but between whom I didn't know.

"I'm talking to Ellie," I snapped. "I don't *need* to do anything."

We'd drawn a crowd; I could sense a group forming a half circle behind me, but I didn't care. I wasn't leaving till I got a straight answer, nontourage be damned.

"Not here, not like this," said Ellie. "We'll talk later, okay?"

Between her and Ryder, people were lining up to talk to me later. Trouble was, I wanted answers *tonight.* "Just tell me why it's over," I begged.

She glanced at our audience, uncomfortable. "You changed," she said.

"How did I change?" I said, daring to inch closer.

"Well," she said, "for one thing, you started drinking."

The flask was not helping matters; it weighed heavy in my hand even though it was nearly empty.

"I only started drinking because you left me. That's not the reason." I moved closer, contemptuously. "Is it because of him? Are you with *Fred* now?" Maria was right; names could be used as insults, so long as they had the right target.

I gave Fred a quick push against the railing.

"Charlie, stop," Ellie cried, and I backed off, hands up and open, my flask gripped loosely by my thumb and forefinger.

I redirected my attention to her. "A *lincoln-douglas?* Really? After *me?*"

It was a lame-ass move, and I knew it. Even in my booze-addled state I knew it. Our school traffics in labels, but that was never Ellie's currency.

She was looking over my shoulder; she was already done. "Bridget, would you take him home? He's not safe to drive."

Unbeknownst to me, Bridget had followed me to the balcony, and she happily accepted the task. "Told you not to make a scene," she purred in my ear. "Keys?"

"You're not driving me anywhere," I spat.

"Charlie," said Ellie, stepping toward me and holding out her perfect palm.

I handed them over, and she walked past me, past the rubberneckers, and into the kitchen to place my keys in a dish.

In the passenger seat of Bridget's Chevy convertible, I dialed Ellie's cell and poured my heart out until her voice mail cut me off. I redialed, and it said her mailbox was full. I chucked my cell onto the backseat and banged my fist on the dashboard and generally had a little fit.

When I was done, Bridget was staring at me with her big cave eyes.

"That was the craziest voice mail I ever heard."

"Be glad it wasn't meant for you, then," I snapped.

"I'm jealous, actually."

"Then you match the light," I slurred, pointing ahead.

"What?"

"Green means go. And I'm the drunk one?"

Wind shook the car, making Bridget clutch the wheel and struggle to stay in the right lane.

We have serious gusts of wind year-round. It's the distinguishing characteristic of Palm Valley, the daily traffic warning on the electronic billboards that light up the 14 Freeway. It'd be nice to see "Coyote Attack" or "Child Abduction" messages every once in a while instead, just to mix things up.

"High Winds Ahead" loses its luster once you realize the wind's never going to be high enough to carry you away and drop you someplace else, like on the other side of the San Gabriel Mountains.

"You better not vom in my car," said Bridget direly. "Especially not over Ellie Chen."

"Can I vom over your driving?"

"Smart move, by the way, giving Ellie your keys so you'd have an excuse to talk to her tomorrow at school."

"She already told me she'd talk to me."

Bridget gave me a look like, *You naive little boy.* "Suuuure."

We drove in merciful silence through downtown, past the civic center. The windows of all the buildings were dark, like eyes shut against the world. Maybe they were pretending they were somewhere else—different buildings in different towns, where perhaps the sun didn't shine as much, but when it did, it meant it in a way it never seemed to mean it here.

Bridget felt the need to reminisce about our past. "Ellie never thanked me, you know. Not even once."

"For what?"

"Teaching you how to use your tongue sophomore year."

"Maybe you taught me too well."

"What do you mean?"

"That's the only thing she ever wanted to do."

"You dated a year and you didn't have sex?" Bridget said.

"Eight months." I frowned. "You seem to know a lot about our relationship."

"I keep tabs on my exes."

"How? Alphabetically? Or is it like counting sheep?"

"You're funny when you're drunk," she remarked. "Funny and bitter. I keep tabs on the ones that *matter*."

"Aw," I said sarcastically.

Bridget was still running around the nostalgia track. "Charlie Dixon, soccer hottie. Why did we break up again?"

"You dumped me because I wouldn't put out," I reminded her.

"That's right. You weren't fast enough," Bridget said, and chuckled. "Hey, I just thought of something. If you and Ellie didn't do it, that means you're still a virgin." She reached over and ruffled my hair. I gripped her wrist and returned it to her lap.

"So?" I said. "She is, too."

Bridget smiled, slowly and deliberately. "You sure about that?"

"Knock it off."

"I hear Fred's a skilled orator ..."

"You heard wrong."

But I wasn't so sure.

We reached the street between our two driveways. My heart was a lead ball, rolling downhill. I felt sick. What if Ellie *had* moved on? (Worse, what if she'd moved on *before* she dumped me?) I couldn't move. I was back in Café Kismet, paralyzed.

Bridget leaned over, all the way over, to undo my seat belt, and this somehow involved her breasts brushing against my chest. Her lips hovered above mine. They were dark red, luscious, and wet. Unlike Ellie's, they would definitely leave a lipstick mark.

"Come inside? For old times' sake?" she said.

"Why so chummy tonight?" I wondered.

She was straddling me now and I placed my hands on her hips to keep her at bay. I honestly couldn't figure out how we'd gotten into this position.

"I waited a long time for you guys to break up," she said.

It was flattering to think she regretted losing me, but she was being awfully friendly for someone who hadn't bothered to wave back when I saw her outside her house last month. Something wasn't right.

"Well, this is my stop." I gripped her arms and tried to dislodge her without hurting her. "Can you, um, move?"

"Sure." She smiled devilishly and started a slow grind with her hips. "How's that?"

"Come on, Bridge, get off my lap."

"So I'm Bridge again, huh?" The swiveling continued.

"I mean it."

"Or what?" she asked.

If I couldn't have Ellie, I didn't want anyone.

"Bridge, Bridge, Bridge," I said, tapping her nose with each name, "I needed to learn with you so I could impress *her*. You were nothing to me but a *bridge* to Ellie." It was a dirty rotten lie, but it got the desired effect: she slapped me so hard my face burned. It felt like the perfect coda to a horrible evening.

"What do you think she's learning from Fred right now?" Bridget whispered nastily. "Make no mistake, Dix, it was you and me in the beginning and it'll be you and me at the end," she added, before slipping out the driver's side and slamming the door. She pulled her jacket up around her neck like a cape against the wind.

It was still early, only nine. I walked next door to my house. The den light was on. My parents were watching *Flip That House*. I pushed the door open so they could see me nod goodnight.

"We didn't hear the garage," Dad said, pausing the TV. "Where's the car?"

"I had too much to drink. Bridget dropped me off," I said in a rare moment of stark honesty. I'd recently—as in two seconds ago—settled on a new diplomatic policy with my parents. It meant not only would I rip off the Band-Aid, I'd set it on fire and throw it at them.

"Maybe we shouldn't have let him have all that wine at Christmas," Mom wondered. "Maybe he developed a taste for it."

"I don't think the kids at the party were drinking *wine*," Dad replied.

Okay, yeah, in desperation, I'd tried to appreciate wine over Christmas break. It flowed easily at holiday parties, and my parents thought it was better to treat alcohol casually, let me have a glass here and there "in moderation," rather than act like it was forbidden and drive me into its arms.

I never gave them any trouble, so I think they felt it was a reward.

When I'd brushed my teeth on Christmas Eve after two glasses of Cabernet, I'd expected to spit out a mouthful of red, but the residue was black, like I'd been chewing black licorice all night, or like tar was building up in me, like the problem wasn't liquor at all, but something inside me that turned everything black.

These were not the kinds of things I could talk to my parents about.

"Who throws a party on a Sunday night, anyway?" Mom asked.

"Maybe Sunday is the new Saturday," Dad teased.

Their diplomatic policy toward me, it seemed, hadn't changed; which is to say it was conducted over and around me, like the first stage of a science project: hypothesis and counterhypothesis, for each other's ears alone. My life was an amusing petri dish they liked to observe, and occasionally poke a stick into. What will he do in Scenario A? What if the conditions are changed? Will he go nuts?

"Do I need to be here for this, or can I go?" I asked, pointing to the hallway with my thumb.

"I'm proud of you for getting a ride," said Dad, refocusing on me. "And you know you can always call us if there aren't any designated drivers. No questions asked."

The idea of Bridget being my designated driver was minorly hilarious.

Flip That House was frozen on screen, impatient. Without my parents' attention, the house remained unflipped. The show didn't exist without them watching it, just like I didn't exist without Ellie as my girlfriend. Unbeknownst to her, Bridget had spent the last few minutes trying to make out with antimatter.

I felt nauseous and dizzy as I crawled into bed. In lieu of brushing my teeth, I swallowed more of my Christmas present from Granddad and swished it around in my mouth. Alcohol kills germs better than toothpaste anyway, right?

All warmth had left me, and I was back to hating the way liquor tasted. Mom's theory was wrong: I hadn't developed a taste for *anything*. That's why I usually covered it up with coffee, juice, or soda. The sharp acid burn of whiskey dirties up everything it comes into contact with, and there's something satisfying about that. I mean, here's a substance that can never be fully absorbed; it will ruin everything you add it to, and it's never the opposite: the thing you add it to, however vast, cannot make it right. One part per million, and it's the one part that has all the power.

It made sense, though. I mean, I wasn't drinking to *enjoy* myself; I was doing it to get through the day.

I wished it had been Ellie who'd slapped me. At least that would mean she still had feelings for me. She always wore those chunky rings she designed herself in jewelry class. They made her fingers look even more delicate, and they would've destroyed my cheek.

Everyone at Maria Posey's party probably thought I was a lush, but there was nothing sloshed or lush or liquid about me.

I lived in the Mojave Desert. I was dehydrated. I was drying out more and more each day, and quenching my thirst with salt water.

At six a.m. on Monday, two deputies from the Palm Valley sheriff's department came to our house and said a girl named Maria Salvador had been dropped off at the Palm Valley ER a few hours ago.

She was alive but in critical condition, hallucinating out of her mind and speaking gibberish. She'd overdosed on LSD and entered a dissociative fugue state. They suspected she'd been given five times the normal dose.

Not surprisingly, her parents wanted answers. According to them, she never would have taken acid, or any other drug, voluntarily. Someone had drugged her. The best and only suspect so far was the dude who'd dropped her off.

Dad was confused, and asked the deputies how we could help. What he meant was, "Why are you here?"

The answer to his unspoken question quickly became known.

My car had been caught on hospital security cameras, dumping the girl and peeling away from the curb. It was then discovered in a ditch by the 14 Freeway. The license plate led the sheriff's department right to my door.

It was a frame job, clean and clear.

In my hungover sleep deprivation, I could only manage a few thoughts:

1. Who was Maria Salvador?

2. Would she be okay?

3. Why hadn't anyone tried to frame me for something sooner?

THERE ARE NO PALM TREES
IN PALM VALLEY

AND THERE NEVER WERE.

In the 1880s, a bunch of Europeans settled here by mistake. They were trying to reach the Pacific Ocean, and believed the existence of palm trees meant they were close to the water. What they were really seeing were Joshua trees, named by the Mormons for the way the branches seem to be reaching up toward God in prayer.

I think the trees are begging God for rain, and He's saying no.

You'd think that once people recognized the error they'd stop coming to Palm Valley, but a hundred and thirty years later, here we all are, putting up golf courses and water parks in the desert and pretending it's normal.

Palm Valley's a charter city, which means we've gone rogue. We have our own constitution, and citizens vote directly on all local decisions, so when Palm Valley High was labeled a failing school in 2007, the city council hired a private corporation called Fresh Start to fix everything.

My mom's the regional director of Fresh Start, which is why we moved here from New Mexico when I was in sixth grade.

The first thing Mom did was fire all the teachers, even those on the tenure track, and make them reapply for their jobs. Half didn't make the cut, so they were swiftly replaced by recent grads who were okay with signing yearly contracts that could be revoked at any time. Good-bye, union. Good-bye, benefits.

Everyone in Palm Valley got whiplash, like, "Huh? When we voted for this proposition, we didn't think it would, like, *change* anything. Betrayal!"

You know how in movies from the '60s people always get bricks thrown in their windows by a hostile, dangerously ignorant populace? That happened to us a few times. We were prank-called constantly and had to get an unlisted number. I used to worry about my mom whenever she left for work; protestors and former teachers screamed and spat at her every morning for the entire summer.

It wasn't just her they went after. While my dad was at work, his car got egged and vandalized, mainly because of where it was parked: the Lambert College faculty lot. His very existence was a traitorous insult to the school system; how could he put up with my mother's hard-line stance when he, too, was a teacher? Nay, a *professor*.

After my parents got a death threat in the mail, we were assigned our own protection, Deputy Sheriff Thompson. Mom and Dad always had a hot thermos of coffee and a plate of dinner waiting for Thompson when his shift started, but he rarely accepted. His wife and brother used to teach at Palm Valley High.

That was the thing—everyone knew someone who'd been affected by the layoffs.

As for me, the brakes on my bicycle got cut when I left it outside Rosati's pizza. I ate gravel on the ride home, had to fling myself sideways to the curb when I realized there was no way to stop. If I'd been on a steeper hill, I might've broken my neck.

While sitting on the curb, recovering from my fall, I watched my bike get run over by a semi. I never asked my parents to replace it.

By the time I was in eighth grade, my mom's decisions had been vindicated: Test scores and graduation rates were way up, and she was suddenly embraced as a positive force in the community.

Part of me couldn't accept that the harassment was over. When you spend a couple years looking over your shoulder and worrying about whether your mom will come home at night, the fear doesn't go away so easily. I guess I kept waiting for the other Converse to drop; for someone who'd been lurking on the sidelines to strike at me. And now, it seemed, someone had.

BLACKMAILERS DON'T DO HOMEWORK

I WAS SHAKING INSIDE, BUT I TRIED TO SOUND CALM AS I explained to Palm Valley's Finest that I'd left my car down the hill from Maria Posey's place and gotten a ride home from my next-door neighbor. My parents repeatedly insisted I'd been home since nine last night.

"We know the exact time because he interrupted our viewing of *Flip That House* when he came in," added Mom, with an assured smile in my direction, but I guess that wasn't good enough for the deputies; they figured Mommy and Daddy would say anything to protect me, and also that I could've snuck out and made my way back to the party later.

I found myself wishing it were Deputy Thompson who'd come to question us. At least we knew him, and toward the end of his three-month stint protecting us, he'd regularly taken us up on dinner. He and I had even kicked a soccer ball around outside a couple times, since my dad's not much of an athlete.

I hadn't seen Thompson in a few years, but I figured he was still around. Palm Valley was that kind of place. Since there was no reason to live here, there was no reason to leave; if you had someplace better to go, you'd have gone there in the first place.

The badges wanted to know where I'd been from midnight to three in the morning, and whether I owned a Flynn Scientific baseball cap. A blurred figure in his late teens or early twenties, wearing a Flynn Scientific cap, could apparently be seen on the hospital security tape.

My parents said no way could anyone search my room without a warrant. They even crossed their arms simultaneously and made a sort of roadblock in front of the stairs. I was impressed. I was so accustomed to their competitive psychobabble about my evolution as a person that I'd forgotten how they'd join forces against outside threats. We were an insulated group; I was protected from all angles.

The deputies grilled me about who else was at the party. I said I didn't remember.

"You'd better hope Ms. Salvador doesn't die, or these charges are going to become much more serious," one of the uniforms told me.

I decided I did remember after all. Maybe I should've felt loyalty and kept my trap shut, but loyalty to whom? *Someone* at the party had swiped my keys and set me up. Ellie had placed them in a dish in the kitchen once I'd handed them over to her.

I gave the badges a truncated guest list, emphasizing Ellie's new squeeze, Fred, and removing my pal Ryder, who'd left the party shortly after I arrived.

The deputies refused to give us information about the condition of my car, but since it was in their custody while they dusted it for prints, Dad had to drive me to school.

We had a decent chat on the way. One-on-one, my parents weren't bad. When they tried to outdo each other narrating and interpreting my actions, they drove me crazy. That's when I turned into "he." ("He probably meant this." "He probably feels that.") *He probably wants to die. He probably wishes he had a sibling.*

But minus their dueling "Explanation of Charlie" act, performed nightly from eight to ten, they were okay.

"I don't want you to worry about this, son," Dad said firmly in his closing remarks as we reached the drop-off lane at Palm Valley High. "You just worry about your schoolwork today. I know you didn't have anything to do with this poor girl's situation. Your mother and I both know that. And I don't think it's going to come to this, but we'll hire a lawyer if we need to."

Dad's always been pretty easygoing in a crisis. Back when Mom was being vilified by the town for her work with Fresh Start, he got trotted out at press conferences like the pro-choice wife of a pro-life politician, as if to say, "My fellow Americans, I'm one of you, so if I can love the senator, you can, too. Be not scared or pissed." He was always good at calming down the crowd, and his status as an award-winning journalism professor helped as well.

"What about Amelia?" I asked. Amelia was my car. Granddad and Ellie and everyone else thought I'd named her for Amelia Earhart, and I let them think so. Dad was the only person who knew the truth about my car's name, and the secret was safe with him.

"If she's in bad shape, we'll just file the insurance claim. That's what it's there for, right?" Dad said.

I was numb. "Right."

"And maybe this goes without saying, but now that the holidays are over, no more drinking."

"Not even in moderation?" I teased.

His smile was thin. "Not even then."

"Hey, Granddad's the one who gave me the flask," I pointed out.

"It was a family heirloom. And times were different when he was growing up."

I nodded shortly, acutely aware of the spiked thermos of coffee in my backpack.

"What do you say we catch *Blood of Mars* this week?" Dad said. "There's a preview on Wednesday night. Could take your mind off things."

When I was younger, Dad and I bonded over sci-fi movies and TV shows. We watched everything from *Star Trek: Next Generation* reruns to *Battlestar Galactica* and *Starship Troopers*. We went to the comic store every Wednesday, when new issues of *X-Men* arrived, and spent an hour perusing our favorite titles.

But that was before we moved to Palm Valley, and I'd had to reinvent myself as an athlete to survive.

As for *Blood of Mars*, I'd been planning to take Ellie's little brother, Jonathan, to the sneak preview. By indulging his own nerdish qualities without revealing my own, I'd scored massive points with Ellie. In her view, it was even sweeter for me to provide this act of charity, considering I was a jock who supposedly couldn't tell a Klingon from a Na'vi and loathed being around anyone who could.

"Can I get back to you on that?" I asked Dad.

He clapped his hand on my shoulder. "Of course. Go get 'em today."

It felt good hearing that my dad didn't suspect me. I'd been pretty sure he didn't, but having proof of his unconditional trust was still nice.

I had library duty first thing, so I slid behind the information desk and logged on to the school server to check the Web site of the local paper, the *Palm Valley Register*. They jam our smartphones on campus (another one of my mom's initiatives), but the library's connection is sound.

To save money, the school has our librarian only come in three days a week, and the rest of the time the staff consists of senior monitors like me and a rotating schedule of volunteer teachers.

The sun had risen just high enough to cast slanted lines on my desk through the blinds. Part of my body was in light and part in shadow.

My library gig was punishment for an altercation in the stairwell last November. I'd caught a creeper named Carl trying to look up girls' skirts. I'd stomped his camera and shoved him against the wall but stopped short of actually hurting him; Ellie hated violence. No witnesses came forward against me because the girls who saw were all happy I'd done it. In retrospect, I should've noticed Ellie wasn't among my supporters. Maybe that's when things started to go sour.

Despite the lack of witnesses, Carl had evidence on his side, in the form of cracked camera equipment—a piece of which was lodged in my soccer cleats. I didn't mind doing time because the library sounded like peace and quiet. For the most part, it was. My shift didn't officially start for another twenty minutes, and I enjoyed the solitude.

The local crime blotter had been updated with a cursory mention of my troubles. Maria Salvador's parents urged anyone with information on their daughter's overdose to come forward. She was eighteen, so they included her name and photo, culled from last year's yearbook. With a pang of regret, I realized she was the sad girl with the dark eyes from the party. Guess she'd found that tragedy she was looking for. Should I have talked to her? Asked her what was making her so sad?

She was in choir with Maria Posey, but Maria Salvador looked nothing like her blond, blue-eyed namesake.

"We call them *Sound of Music* Maria and *West Side Story* Maria," said a wry voice.

I looked up. Bridget. She was flushed and a little out of breath. "If we're feeling generous, that is," she added. "Most of the time we call them Maria and Other Maria."

"Why don't you call them by their last names? That's what guys would do."

She looked at me like I was stupid. "Because then no one would feel bad."

She tossed my cell phone onto the desk. It bounced once, and I winced before pocketing it.

"You left this in my car last night. Threw it, actually," said Bridget. "Before calling me a starter girlfriend."

She was a hangover's hangover: annoying in and of herself as well as a reminder of my own less-than-chivalrous behavior the evening before. I took a deep breath. "Sorry for what I said last night. I didn't mean it, about using you to get to Ellie. I was drunk."

She picked up my dirty coffee, took a sip, and made a face. "You're still drunk. Do you mean what you're saying now?"

"I'm less drunk. I'm 73.5 percent sober," I said. "And I *am* sorry for what I said. What we had—it was fun, I just wasn't ready—"

She rolled her eyes. "I know. It's okay."

"Then why'd you slap me?"

"I don't know. I've never slapped anyone before. I thought it might be fun."

"Was it?" I asked, with an edge.

She laughed. "See, this, right here, is why I couldn't be with you. It's not because you didn't want to have sex sophomore year. I mean, that's part of it. It's because you're always apologizing. The boy who got drunk and spiteful last night? Him, I like. But you . . . We're just not a good fit when you're regular you."

Glad to have that over with, I jerked my head toward the computer screen. "You think *West Side Story* Maria's gonna be okay?" (I refused to call her "Other Maria.")

Bridget shrugged. "She took a *lot* of LSD. I hear it messes with your spine, and sticks there, and you could have flashbacks, for, like, years."

"A spine is somewhat vital," I agreed. I'd read in the paper that a dissociative fugue state causes loss of identity, and could last days or even months. It sounded horrifying.

"She knew the risks."

I was taken aback. "Harsh. I thought you songbirds all flocked together in a loving V-formation."

"You and your soccer buddies always see jock-to-jock?" she countered.

"Well, yeah."

"Okay, here's my official reaction." Eyes wide, emeralds aglitter, breathy voice: "'It's awful what happened. I can barely function.'" She grinned. "That's what I'm telling the sheriff's department later."

"You're talking to them later?"

"Everyone is. Everyone at the party, anyway. I just passed the front office, and I heard Jeffries agree to let them interrogate people all day as long as parents are present. The stay-at-home round-robin emergency callers have never been this wet."

I took a sip of my spiked coffee. I'd felt I deserved it after my personal visit from the authorities this morning.

"It was my car that dropped her at the hospital after the

overdose," I said carefully, hardly believing the words as they fell out of my mouth. "Apparently, I barely hit the brakes before peeling away. May as well have the word 'guilty' spray painted on the hood."

Her eyes widened again, taking up even more of her face, which I didn't think was possible. "They think *you* did it? No way."

"Yeah. I might have to lawyer up." My hands shook.

"Wow, Dix. You suddenly got interesting again."

"Fuck off," I said mildly. "They'll dust the car for prints and find someone else's on top of mine, and I'll be home free," I added, with a bravado I didn't possess. "*And*, once she stops hallucinating, she'll tell everyone it wasn't me."

"*If* she stops hallucinating. I heard an urban legend once, about a drug messenger who kept the product in his sock. It seeped through to his skin, several tabs of it, and sent him to the asylum."

"I stopped listening at 'urban legend,'" I lied.

"There's not much you can do to clear your name."

"Everyone at the party saw you give me a ride in your car," I protested.

"No, they saw you give your keys to Ellie. No reason you couldn't have come back to the party later. No one's gonna stick their neck out for you, not when it'll help deflect blame from *them*."

If Bridget felt any sympathy for me, she was extremely good at hiding it. She flipped a chair around and straddled it, propping her elbows onto the information desk. "Anyway. Enough chitchat. I'm here because I need your help."

I frowned. "With what?"

"Friday morning I left my flash drive in one of the computers here, and when I came back to grab it, it was gone."

"What's on it?"

"Only my college application essay." She groaned. "Someone stole it! And now all they have to do is replace my name with theirs and they're golden. They can snake my spot at some school and no one will ever know."

I walked out from behind the information desk and motioned for Bridget to sit with me at an empty table.

"Did you check all the computers?" I said.

"Yes, *Dix*, I checked all the computers," she said, insulted. "It's not here." She pointed to the left. "I was seated in the corner by the window."

"You checked your backpack, your locker—"

"Do I look like a child?"

Um. Definitely not. "When were you here?"

"Second period."

I chewed on my pen cap for a second. "For study hall?"

"Yes. I was editing my essay, smoothing out the rough spots, rearranging sentences. I had *everything* else for my application done and ready to go. If I can't find it, I'll be stuck getting a bachelor of arts at frigging Lambert."

She knew full well that's where I was going. "You'll always be B.S. material to me, Bridge."

"Cute."

"You didn't back up the file?"

"No."

"Not at home, not on e-mail?"

"Are you trying to make me feel worse? Because you're really good at it."

"I'm good at a lot of things," I remarked. "Or did you forget?"

She smirked. "Only because I taught you. I didn't back it up, okay? I was stupid. But I need that essay."

"Can't you rewrite it or something?"

"*Oh* my *God*. Do you understand what a college essay *is*? It's all amorphous nonsense. But I had the nonsense exactly how I wanted it, and I can't re-create a month's work in four days! The deadline for UC Irvine is Friday!"

"The deadline for UC Irvine was November 30th. Try again."

"Okay, jeez. Make me say it: The essay's for a scholarship. Happy now? If I don't get my essay back, I won't be *going* to college."

"Look, if you did leave your flash drive behind, *anyone* could've taken it," I said.

"I know. That's why I need your help. You can access the log-ins, right? Find out who was here second period?"

For a while, people were stealing books off the shelves, so now everyone who came into the library had to swipe their student ID card as they walked in, even if they didn't plan on checking out anything.

I shook my head. "It only tells me their ID number; it doesn't say who it belongs to."

She waved that issue away. "I know a guy who can translate those. So you'll help me, right?"

Bridget leaned in, allowing me a glimpse down her full-to-bursting blouse. Her leg rubbed against mine beneath the table, like a matchstick looking to ignite, and she implored me with her huge green eyes.

"Tell me this," I said. "All that stuff you piled on thick last night, about waiting for me to be single again? Did you really want to get back together, or did you just think if we were back together, I'd help you find your flash drive today?"

"I figured it couldn't hurt," she admitted. "I saw you at the party, remembered you worked at the library, and thought I'd sweeten you up before springing a favor on my once-and-future boyfriend."

"I *could* help," I said slowly, shaking her loose and standing up, "but why would I?"

"You'd do it for Ellie," she pouted.

I stared her straight in the eyes, just so there was no mistaking what I was about to say, and the degree to which I meant it. "I would do *anything* for Ellie."

She looked genuinely hurt for a second. "So the answer's no?"

"The answer's no. I've got too much going on with soccer. We have a big game Friday against Agua Dulce."

Bridget stared at me for a second. "Hmm," she said. "I was afraid of this."

My hands started shaking again. "Of what?"

"Of you refusing. Go ahead and take a look at your cell phone."

I felt a slow, icy dread crawl up my spine. "What do you mean?"

"Look at your text message history," she articulated calmly.

I took out my phone and sat back down. Tapped the messages icon and scrolled through it.

There were twenty texts from Bridget to me, all time-stamped from last night. That wasn't the horrifying part. The horrifying part was the twenty texts from *me* to *her* in return.

Apparently, I was bringing sexy back. In explicit detail.

"Find my flash drive by the scholarship deadline Friday afternoon, or Ellie gets an eyeful," said Bridget.

"You're blackmailing me!"

"You didn't give me a choice."

I clenched my fist beneath the table. "She dumped me. Why would she care?"

"*You* care, though, don't you? You think you still have a chance."

Her smugness knew no bounds. She wasn't the cat who ate the canary—she was the cat who bred canaries in captivity and force-fed them to *each other*, then had a foie gras–style feast off one epic, stuffed bird.

I shook my head, incredulous. "You sat there in your room all night, pretend-sexting me, and using my phone to write back?"

"It's pretty basic, Dix. But thanks, I thought it was clever."

I laughed for like two hours. Leaned back in my seat and clasped my hands behind my head.

It made her nervous. "What? Why are you laughing?"

"You stupid, horrible . . . I could hate-kiss you."

"What?"

"You've given me an alibi!"

It took her a second to realize I was right.

"Show these to the sheriff's deputy. *Don't* show them to Ellie," I ordered.

Bridget's dark red lips parted in a wide smile, exposing her teeth. "Guess that means you're helping me."

I guessed it did.

RULES OF ENGAGEMENT

AFTER MOM'S TRIUMPH WITH FRESH START, MY PARENTS could've moved on to the next town to work their magic, but Granddad enjoyed having us nearby, and my dad enjoyed his position teaching at Lambert College. Plus, I think they wanted to keep me in the district to prove Fresh Start was a success: "Look! Palm Valley has such a wondrous school system now, we want our *own* kid to attend. We would never dream of leaving!"

What my mom and Fresh Start failed to comprehend was that the teachers were only half the problem. The real reason everyone had been bombing tests and never participating in class was because they were terrified of upperclassmen. The bullying of freshmen and sophomores was a religion and a sport, with the combined zealotry of each.

If, as a fourteen- or fifteen-year-old, you're constantly calculating which route in the hallway is least likely to lead to disfigurement or dismemberment, or wondering who'll steal and destroy your homework assignment, piss in your lunch bag, "decorate" your locker, or follow you home for more secluded beatings, it's tough to give a crap about your grades.

So how do you stop bullying? By giving everyone a group to

run with; a group to call home; a group to protect them. From the moment freshmen arrive now, they belong to something. A team. A program. An after-school extracurricular.

The second to last week of eighth grade, boosters from the high school show up in the parking lot to recruit prospects. Competition is fierce. Over the summer you can change your mind, but you have to have something else lined up, or someone to swap with who won't stab you in the back at the last second. The first, best, and only hope for survival is to claim an identity as quickly as possible before stepping on campus.

It doesn't really matter what you choose; it just matters *that* you choose, or else you'll be orphaned and labeled a nomad, ripe for exploitation and daily beatings, and no one—I mean, no one— can protect you.

Upperclassmen aren't supposed to interact with freshmen or sophomores unless they have permission from your group. Anyone who violates this rule is subject to lawless vengeance, appropriate to the size of the violation and the temperament of the group that's been provoked.

The library is no-man's-land, and by junior year the rules loosen up a little. Senior year, anyone in your class can interact unless the leader of a group's put out an injunction against you.

As head songbird, *Sound of Music* Maria could've banned me from her party, but I think she found it entertaining to watch me flounder and drown.

It was obvious who your group was. You moved in packs,

between classes, before school, after school, on the weekends. Without a group, you were a sitting duck.

Ryder Lennox was the most gifted athlete at Tumbleweed Junior High. He was a shoo-in for any sport, in high school and beyond. We became friends during sixth-grade Little League, but we both chose soccer for our group freshman year of high school.

I was accepted to the team no problem, but Ryder got orphaned from sports after failing the drug test. With no one to protect him, he spent all his time fending off attacks from upperclassmen. One-on-one he might've been okay, but the fights were always lopsided. I tried to help him, but I was tied up in soccer every day. If I walked with him in the hall, bullies had to leave us alone or face the wrath of every cleat and beckham, but Ryder hated having a babysitter, hated relying on anyone.

My parents tried to intervene, too. They offered to let Ryder live with us for a while, but that just made the situation worse. Things got ugly with Ryder's mom. She felt really insulted, like we'd been saying she wasn't good enough to take care of Ryder, but it was his older brother, Griffin, we were worried about. He'd dropped out, and was urging Ryder to do the same. I wouldn't have blamed Ryder if he'd done just that.

I asked him once, "*How could you do it? How could you mess up your whole high school life by taking drugs the first week of school, when you knew they'd have the test?*" He just told me I didn't understand.

We drifted apart. Ryder barely showed up at school. When he

did, he got jumped, and the longer he stayed away, the worse his return would be. He was hospitalized twice.

And then one day, spring of freshman year, the beatings stopped. I wanted to ask what had changed, but he wasn't exactly forthcoming, and I was so relieved he was okay that I didn't push it.

Sophomore year, I got a girlfriend—Bridget—and by then Ryder and I barely saw each other. Junior year, I got a second girlfriend—Ellie—and we hung out even less. Then last August he asked me if I wanted to make some easy cash.

I should've said no.

I should've done a lot of things.

A FAVOR FOR A FRIEND

I LOGGED IN TO THE LIBRARY SYSTEM AND PRINTED OUT THE ID numbers of everyone who'd been there second period on Friday. Bridget promised to meet with her source and give me a list of their names by the end of the day. She was due at choir rehearsal right when school let out, and I had history last period, so she told me she'd place the names in an envelope and tape them to the underside of the desk closest to the window.

At lunch, I took my usual spot at the soccer table, next to Patrick Penrose, the head of our group and also our goalie. He was tall and kind of bulky, muscular but not so much a brick house as a mud house that swayed and leaned with the wind. Soccer balls stuck to him; he had an uncanny ability to put himself in their path. Off the field he was pretty chill, but he took the game seriously and he was determined to keep a clean sheet this season to impress college scouts.

Patrick was always organizing trips to Maxwell Park and Wildwater Kingdom. His cousin worked there and helped us bypass the endless lines by calling ahead on his walkie-talkie, claiming our last ride had broken down and shooting us straight to the front. For this he was rewarded with "superior customer service" pay bumps each quarter.

I opened my thermos of coffee and took a swallow. It was cold now, but it was still tinged with the hair of the dog that had bit me and hadn't let go since Ellie ditched me at Café Kismet.

There seemed no reason to sober up today. I'd been framed, blackmailed, and presented with a false alibi, all before noon.

"Top it up?" Josh said quietly, waggling a miniflask under the table.

I was surprised. I didn't think Josh liked me. When I got moved to defense this season, Josh was bumped to second string. I used to play center forward, the glory position, sort of the equivalent of quarterback in football, but coach had decided my particular skill set was better utilized elsewhere.

Now we were both fullbacks, but Josh only got to play if I needed a break or got benched for fouling someone, and he resented me for it. In contrast, I never gave Delinsky, my own replacement for center forward, a hard time. The game was the game. Maybe this was Josh's way of making peace and saying there were no hard feelings anymore?

I accepted the offering and drunkenly observed my fellow classmates for the rest of the hour.

The sheriff's deputies didn't even try to be discreet. They called someone new out of the cafeteria every two minutes. I enjoyed Fred's perp walk in particular; it was probably the most terrifying moment of his life.

I probably should've jotted down the names of everyone who was summoned, because one of them had driven my car and dumped *West Side Story* Maria at the hospital, but I was too out of it to think clearly, and I was bracing myself for my follow-up interrogation.

The strange thing was, nobody seemed to care about Maria Salvador. Or at least, no one was talking about her. Every conversation I overhead was about how "annoying" and "unfair" it was that the final college-counseling sessions had to be rescheduled to accommodate the investigation into her overdose.

Palm Valley High was a cold-ass place, but it was not without irony: the conscientious people who'd set up their college meetings for today would get screwed, and the slackers like me, who'd signed up later in the week, wouldn't be affected.

I stumbled into history class early, dehydrated and fighting off a headache, and sure enough Bridget's envelope was there, under the desk by the window. The location she'd picked was perfect because on Monday nights for the last several months I always did a favor for Ryder. All I had to do was make sure the window was unlocked when I left, and on Tuesday he'd give me forty dollars. Easiest money I ever made.

Most of the time it was a cinch, but every once in a while I ran into trouble, like maybe a kid stayed late to talk to Mr. Donovan, or Mr. Donovan himself lingered to organize the supply closet, in which case I was supposed to draw a small red X on the back of

Ryder's lock with a wax pencil as I passed by his locker on my way out.

Today was an easy day—I unlocked the window before anyone else arrived—and I was happy for it, until I remembered I had no one to spend the forty dollars on, not anymore.

Ellie was only one classroom away, right behind us, but she may as well have been on the moon. I got a sickening thought: had she dumped me because forty dollars wasn't enough to take her to nice places? Just as quickly, I dismissed the theory. We'd been happy before I had any money. We'd been happy going to free events and occasionally watching DVDs with her brother, Jonathan. We'd been happy.

So why did she end it?

Mr. Donovan taught history and served as the debate coach. He was widely regarded as the best teacher at Palm Valley, definitely the best hire of Mom's and a shining example of how to teach "to the test." (Conveniently, Fresh Start also wrote and sold the quarterly tests used to measure whether students were learning above, at, or below their grade levels.) My mom's crowning achievement was tying teacher salaries to performance. If they failed to meet their student achievement quotas, they'd lose pay, and their pet projects, deemed frivolous, would lose funding as well. Donovan's efforts were single-handedly responsible for keeping the debate team alive.

He was the kind of teacher whose enthusiasm made you feel embarrassed for him. He even wore jackets with patches at the elbows, a parody of a professor. It was like, protect yourself, dude. Why do you have to make it easy for us to mock you? Have some self-preservation.

The debate kids (the lincoln-douglases) loved Mr. Donovan, though. They fed off his enthusiasm. It fueled them, and the rest of us couldn't touch them. They were nerds, but they didn't care, because they didn't need our approval or acceptance. They were what the groups were supposed to be but hardly ever were: close-knit, insulated. Tight. And they were this way because they wanted to be, not because of an arbitrary choice they made freshman year that lumped their fates together.

Maybe that's why Ellie had taken up with Fred. Maybe that earnestness appealed to her.

I held my textbook up as a cover and opened the envelope Bridget had left me. The list was thirty people long. I rolled my eyes and glanced at the first four.

Danny: freshman, category unknown. Great. I'd have to figure out which group he ran with and get permission to talk to him.

Sound of Music Maria, head of songbirds: I could talk to her tonight after soccer, during the girls' choir rehearsal. (It didn't hurt that Ellie would be there, too.)

Josh, my fellow beckham: the simplest to approach. He also had history class with me.

Jennifer, consigliere of chekhovs (the tiny, elite group of AP students who studied dead Russian lit. Derogatory nickname: cherkoffs). Bridget had drawn an arrow and written, "She's in my

English class and I saw her trying to crib off my exam last year."
(Doubtful, I thought. It was probably the exact opposite.)

I was already exhausted and bored by the list. My motivation to solve the "Case of the Missing Flash Drive" waned with each passing minute of class. My order of priorities was as follows:

1. Win back Ellie
2. Find out who framed me
3. Win the game against Agua Dulce
56. Laundry
327. Locate Bridget's flash drive

She had me over a barrel, though. Until I'd confirmed that the deputies had bought my fake alibi, and until I erased all the fake sexts from Bridget's phone, I had to at least pretend to help her. We were all faking something, and faking it hard. It should've been the school motto.

Nevertheless, when the bell rang, I darted next door to Ellie's chemistry class to wait for her instead of questioning Josh.

She slipped out of the room and into the throng and I called out to her. Her back stiffened and she kept walking so I scurried to keep up.

The top half of her hair was looped back with bobby pins, almost invisible in her dark hair. I wanted to tug the tendrils loose.

"Ellie, please wait."

"I don't have your keys," she said, and rejoined the exodus.

"I know." I reached out to touch her arm.

She turned to face me, and her shoulders lifted in the smallest of sighs. "I have to go."

"We all have to go. Carry your books?" I said.

I glanced up to see a small smile on her face, like we were in this together, like last night was a battle, but we were on the same side now. We'd been in the trenches but this was us, after the war.

She stepped out of the swarm and hefted her books into my arms. We strode down the hallway together. She smelled like rain, which was impossible. I was just so thirsty.

"How are you feeling?" she said.

"Terrible."

"Too sober?"

"Ha." We reached her locker all too quickly.

"I'm pretty sure I have a gin-soaked rag in here you could suck on," she said, spinning the lock.

I leaned against the lockers and glanced at hers while she opened it. She still had a picture up from Homecoming, taped below her mirror. Our tongues were sticking out. She'd worn a velvet dress, the kind you could draw patterns on in darker shades by stroking it the wrong way, but it was nothing compared to the softness of her hair, which had framed her face in spiraling curls. If I closed my eyes, I could still feel a fistful in my hands.

I envied the Charlie in the picture. He might've been a little insecure, but in the photo he looked stupidly happy, and he had no idea what was right around the corner. What interested me now was happy Ellie's expression. Was she faking it for the camera?

Was she counting the days, minutes, seconds till she could get rid of me? Was the dance a last hurrah to her?

"You want to slug me," I said.

"I'm considering it."

"I wouldn't blame you. In fact, I'd welcome it."

She took her books back from me, placed them in her locker, and turned to regard me. "Crashing Maria's party and calling me out? Really?"

I looked down, embarrassed. "I know."

"Why are you drinking so much?" she asked softly, no more sarcasm.

"You know why," I mumbled.

"You can't blame this on me."

"I'm not. For some, hell is other people. For me, it's endless reality."

"Try again," she said. "Less Sartre, more you."

"When I'm sober, you definitely broke up with me—right? It's never going to stop being true," I said. "But when I'm drunk, maybe it didn't happen. *Maybe*. And maybe it can be fixed."

"Charlie . . ."

"I drink to forget. And I drink so I can imagine that tomorrow things will be different. If I had to accept reality as the only truth, I'd obliterate."

She turned back to her locker, for no reason, and without doing anything. Her hands eventually lifted to her face and covered her eyes, and we stood there for a moment, not talking.

She had asked the wrong question. Instead of wondering why I'd started drinking, she should've asked, "How come you didn't drink when we were together?" because the answer was simple: I hadn't needed to. Ellie was my drink, and I'd spent the whole time we were dating fearing the moment my glass was going to run out.

Eventually, I forged ahead. "I can't believe you poured me into Bridget's car, *knowing* I was miserable, *knowing* I'd seen you with Fred, *knowing* something could happen with her."

Her eyes flashed. "I was pretty knowledgeable for a three-second conversation, wasn't I?"

"It meant you were testing me or else you didn't care what happened, and either way I couldn't take it."

She let out a strangled noise of frustration. "You think it means I didn't care? Saving you from crashing your car or killing yourself means I *didn't* care?"

It felt good to get a rise out of her, like we were finally at the same level of upset. "I just mean—" I started.

"She lives next door to you, it made sense for her to drive you home, it wasn't a *test*, there was no *subtext*. I just wanted you to get home okay because I still—" she stopped abruptly and my whole body tensed.

"Because you what?"

"Because I still worry about you," she said angrily.

I chose to focus on the words and not the way they were

delivered. I chose to focus on the door that had swung wide open, inviting me back into her life.

"It's only been a couple weeks, Charlie. I can't just shut off my emotions. I don't want you to get in an accident. God."

I let her outburst dissipate and settle in the air around us for a moment.

"Last night, you said I changed. So I'll change back. I'll keep changing or I'll stop, just tell me what to do, tell me what I did wrong," I pleaded.

"I kissed Fred," she blurted out. "It was . . . sloppy. Terrible."

My smile was just as terrible. "I *knew* something was going on between you two."

"But it wasn't. Don't you get it? When you saw us, we really were just talking." She laughed joylessly. "About *school*. About how to get Jonathan into debate next year."

"He's only in seventh grade."

"His teachers think he should skip ahead a year, and he's really freaking out. I promised to make sure he had a group lined up so he doesn't get bullied. Fred said he could help: meet with him before school this week, introduce him to the right people. But then you accused me—in front of everyone! And the fact that you assumed we were together, that you actually thought I'd moved on from you that quickly, pissed me off. So during Spin the Bottle I made sure I ended up with him."

I was angry, but then I was relieved. We'd both messed up, and now we could move forward. Bonus: The kiss had been terrible, reminding her of what she was missing.

"You played Spin the Bottle after I left? Really? That's what songbirds do for kicks at parties?" I teased.

"Well, that and LSD, apparently," she said tonelessly.

My hands shook. "What do you know about that?"

"Not nearly as much as you do."

I was stunned. "What's that supposed to mean?"

She looked at the wall clock. "I'm late for choir."

I followed her. "Talk afterwards?"

She didn't answer, and I stood alone in the hallway like a chump, watching her walk away, no better off than I'd been before our chat.

BAD REPUTATION

FIRST ON MY LIST TO ASK ABOUT THE FLASH DRIVE WAS
other-fullback Josh.

As we walked out to the soccer field for practice, he admitted he'd been at the library second period last Friday but said he left before the bell rang to use the bathroom (which meant he'd left before Bridget and couldn't have stolen her flash drive). I could confirm his story with Patrick, if I wanted. They'd seen each other at the sinks and discussed the upcoming game against Agua Dulce. Josh sounded confident and casual when he told me this, and since we saw Patrick at the same time out on the field, it would've been impossible for him to ask Patrick to lie before I reached him. I mentally crossed Josh off Bridget's list and moved on.

Practice was brutal. I'd been ever so slightly buzzed for several hours over the course of the day, and running drills nearly made me puke. I keeled over twenty minutes in and had to take a break on the bench. Mr. Mitchell, the assistant coach, brought me a bottled water and a face towel and sat down beside me.

"You okay?" he said.

"Yeah, I think I just got that bug that's going around."

"You sure that's all it is? You look pale, like you've lost weight, too."

The all-booze Ellie Diet. "I'll be all right in time for Friday."

"Why don't you take it easy today, hit the showers, and see how you're doing tomorrow. I'd hate to take you out; we could really use you for that game, Charlie." He lowered his voice. "Josh is good, but he's not you."

Josh.

Josh had given me a top-up at lunch, kept me buzzing midway through the day. Was he trying to sabotage me so he'd get to open against Agua Dulce instead of me, maybe even play the whole game?

I'd been playing soccer long enough to know it wasn't exactly what you'd call fair. There's no objective reality to it. The ref either sees you foul someone or he doesn't, and if he doesn't, well, it's like it never happened. I've pushed guys out of the way and flat-out stolen the ball, and they've done the same to me. Everyone does it at some point. Were you offside? Doesn't matter—unless the ref saw. Did the ball bounce over the line into the box and then bounce back out? Doesn't count as a goal—unless the ref saw.

This is supposedly one of the reasons Americans don't like soccer, while the rest of the world shits themselves during the World Cup. The game's existence defies American values: our love of Fairness and the American Dream, which states that anyone who works hard and follows the rules deserves to succeed. Soccer's not like that. Your goal could be wrongly disallowed, your opponent could trip, push, shove, or kick you out of the way without repercussion, and dumb luck could prevail at any moment. The best team might not win. Or it might. (Or it might, *but only in the long run.*) Consistency is still rewarded, though. If you have majority possession of the ball, with solid passing and good strikers, you'll probably win. But only probably.

For me, soccer's randomness was what made the victories so great. Because it didn't have to go that way. It didn't have to go *any* way. So many things in my life felt inevitable, out of my control. (Ellie. College.) This was glorious lunacy, unpredictable bliss.

Until recently I'd been psyched about the regional championship. My rival on Agua Dulce's team was this preppy, floppy-haired, cokehead-looking guy named Steve, and he was a dream to foul. It was especially entertaining to mess with the guy's head; I'd foul him as quickly and ridiculously as possible, and he'd be so enraged he wouldn't be able to concentrate the entire first half.

My team counted on me to get at least a yellow card every other game. It wasn't dirty playing—it was part of our strategy: Charlie brings the rough stuff and takes the hit. I was the drop of liquor in the team's Gatorade, the thing that dirtied us up. If that meant I got kicked out for a few matches each year, it just increased my reputation for the next game, as someone dangerous to watch out for. Some guys spent so much time avoiding me they didn't even try to gain possession.

When I'd played center forward, it was a whole different story.

Then, I was the one trying not to get fouled; I was the one trying to score. But sometimes you have to make do with what you've got.

I showered in the gym building, changed into my regular clothes, and headed back outside. The school was basically on lockdown at night, except for prescheduled club events, so I had to reenter from the front to get to the auditorium.

The school always looked damned depressing at night. It was only four thirty, but it felt much later. From this part of town, the San Gabriel Mountains cut us off from the sun half an hour earlier than at home. The school parking lot was dark and half empty. The windows and doors of the building were dark except for a few beams of light shooting out the front entrance by the auditorium. Inside, all the empty hallways and silent lockers were barely illuminated by tiny floor lights. The classrooms were hollow except for slivers of light sneaking through vertical blinds.

Ryder bumped my shoulder as I walked up the steps toward the double doors. "Hey," he said, ubiquitous cigarette in his mouth, box of orange Tic Tacs in his hand. He quickly slipped the Tic Tacs into his pocket and took a drag off his cigarette.

I wanted to tell him those Tic Tacs weren't going to cover up his smoker's breath; if anything they'd make it worse. And who eats the orange ones, anyway? It's the flavor of antiseptic.

"How was practice?" he said, gazing out at the field.

"Okay."

"Got out kind of early, didn't you?"

It made me feel guilty that he kept track of the practices, even four years later, of the team he should've been on.

"Yeah, Mitchell told me to take it easy tonight."

He patted his pockets. "I don't have your cash on me yet."

"No worries. Tomorrow's fine."

He nodded appreciatively. "Good lookin' out. We still on for lunch tomorrow? I may have a way for you to make more money, if you're interested. A lot more."

I said I definitely was, and then he was off again.

In my dehydrated state, I had a thought: If I saved my forty dollars per week from now until June, I could take Ellie to prom in style. It couldn't hurt to plan ahead, right? Just in case we patched things up between now and then? Maybe it was stupid, but with the extra money he'd just mentioned . . . yeah, maybe it could all work out.

I turned and watched Ryder go, until he merged with the darkness and all that remained of him was the orange glow of the tip of his cigarette.

Why was Ryder at school now, when he hadn't been all day? Maybe he'd finished doing whatever it was he did on Monday nights in the history room, courtesy of my unlocked window, and was making his getaway by strolling out the building in plain sight. I was happy enough making cash here and there, and I didn't want to stick my nose in it. Some things you don't ask and everyone's better off that way.

55

I watched the songbirds' dress rehearsal from the back of the auditorium, and during their fifteen-minute break I snuck backstage and down the stairs, past the makeup room and props storage, all the way back to the dressing rooms. I knocked twice and *Sound of Music* Maria, looking perfectly coiffed in the choir uniform of wine-colored vest, black turtleneck, and black pants, opened the door and scowled at me, like we were still at her party and I was still not invited. "*What.*"

"Who swiped my keys from your place last night?"

"I don't know, and if I did, I'd tell the sheriff's department, not *you.*"

"Can you at least give me the list of guests so I can figure it out for myself? And I'll save you the trouble: yes, I know I wasn't supposed to be there. I guess I had this coming to me, right?"

Bridget appeared behind her. Not the ex I was looking for. As usual. In her choir uniform, Bridget looked like a lusty caterer. She coughed at me. Roughly translated, it meant, "Stay on target."

I glared at her. Roughly translated, it meant, "Drift received."

Bridget held out a box of choir programs for *Sound of Music* Maria's benediction. They were for the upcoming winter concert. "I guess we're going to have to send them back," she said apologetically.

I plucked one from the stack and read the type under the title: "'Soloist: Maria Salvador.' Well! That's awkward."

Maria Posey shoved the box back at Bridget. "Get them reprinted by next Saturday. I can't include these in my college portfolio."

Bridget ducked back into the dressing room. It was strange seeing her all submissive, taking orders.

"You're still going ahead with the concert, even though your soloist is in the hospital?" I asked.

"It's going to be a *fund-raiser* for her."

"How altruistic of you. Why not leave her name on the program, then, as a tribute?"

"Because that would be inaccurate. Did you need something else?"

"Yeah, actually. A flash drive went missing from the library last week. I'm sort of on duty there, so—"

"You mean you were *sentenced* there for breaking Carl's camera under the stairwell. Props, by the way—"

"—so I have to look into it. I heard you were there second period last Friday?"

Maria squinted at me. "What're you, the library police? What kind of flash drive?"

"The kind that holds information," I said sarcastically. "Did you see anything suspicious last Friday or not?"

Her nostrils flared. She didn't answer right away, and then she snapped, "Not that it's any of your business, but I was getting tutoring help from Oscar with my French."

I sucked in my teeth. "Tutoring, huh? And here I thought you were gunning for valedictorian."

"Maybe you should stop. Thinking."

I tried to peer behind her. "Is Ellie back there?"

"She already left," answered Bridget, popping out again. Her Not-Ellie-ness had become an annoying habit of hers. "Come on, I'll drive you."

This didn't seem like a particularly good idea, considering what had almost happened last time I accepted a ride from her, but neither did walking five miles on a shaky stomach. Besides, we had business to discuss.

"Make sure you mention the fund-raiser on your college application. They eat that shit up," I said faux-sincerely to *Sound of Music* Maria.

"Thanks for the tip, *Charlie*."

"You know, I really don't like the way she says my name," I told Bridget outside in the parking lot, my hands shoved in my pockets.

"Imagine spending the past four years with her," Bridget replied.

I shuddered. "Why'd you choose choir, anyway?"

"Poms was full and I wasn't good enough for valley belles." She said it matter-of-factly, without a trace of self-pity, but it made me see her in a new light . . . Bridget wanted to play volleyball but got stuck singing? I'd had no idea.

Some of the beckhams, like Josh, were tools, but at least I'd gotten my first choice in groups. It never occurred to me other people might've been trapped all this time with people they didn't like. Any group was still better than being a nomad, though.

"Maria agreed to help get me in at the last second, on the

condition that I back her on everything and help her rise through the ranks quickly."

"On the condition that you be her slave," I recapped. Maria must've made the same deal with a couple other desperate girls, enabling her to assume the position of head songbird as an underclassman.

"I didn't have a choice," Bridget sniffed.

"So why couldn't *you* talk to her about the flash drive? Why were you hiding in the dressing room while I did all the work?" I asked.

"I don't trust her, but I can't *accuse* her of stealing it. She'd make my life miserable, and we still have five months left of school."

"Fine. How'd it go with the deputies?"

"I think your messages made them blush," she said. "Or maybe they learned something."

I cringed. "Great." I reached for her purse and dug sloppily through it, looking for the ticking time bomb. "So now you can erase every single one. And if you show them to Ellie, if you even allude to them in her presence, you can kiss your essay good-bye."

Bridget raised one perfectly shaped eyebrow. " 'Allude'? Triple word score. Maybe I should just have *you* write my essay."

"I don't think I could accurately mimic your . . . unique voice."

"Why are you so hung up on your precious Ellie? You act like she craps Bazooka Joe gum. Refresh your home page already. She dumped you."

"What do you know about that?" I demanded.

"More than you do, probably," she said, sounding bored. We reached her car and she unlocked it.

"Suppose you tell me what you know, and I tell you what I found out about your flash drive." I ducked inside the car and saw her do the same.

"Well, it's just a rumor . . ."

I was done neutralizing her phone, so I tossed her purse back at her. "I can make up my own rumors. I want facts."

She thought for a second, biting her bottom lip.

I couldn't stand that she might be sitting on information, however inaccurate. "Well?"

"I heard it had something to do with soccer or Ryder," she offered.

I was confused. "Is it like a sixty-forty thing? Which one?"

"I don't know. That's just what I *heard*."

"So it wasn't about college?" I blurted out.

She pounced on that like a piece of candy, practically licking her lips. "Interesting. Why do you ask?"

I'd known for six years I'd be going to Lambert College. My dad's teaching job cuts tuition in half, and I wouldn't need room and board. It was a small liberal arts school with a large new-media endowment. Putting together the forms and signing up was just the last check mark on a very short to-do list. While my classmates scurried like rats, I'd been picked up by an unseen hand and plopped down right at the end of the maze. It was all decided, all finished. Inevitable.

Ellie, on the other hand, wanted to go back East, her old stomping grounds, maybe NYU or Columbia. She told me she would also apply to Lambert, but maybe that was a lie—maybe she'd just been biding her time until she broke up with me. Applications for most of the places on her list had been due last month; was it really a coincidence she'd called it quits with no warning and no explanation right before college plans needed to be finalized?

"You think Ellie dumped you because you'll be going to different schools?" said Bridget.

"Basically."

Lambert's paperwork was due this week. I still didn't know if Ellie had ever sent them her records.

Bridget shrugged. "Could be. *Anyway*. What did you find out about my flash drive? Maria seemed edgy, right?"

"She was hissy because she's supposed to be this genius or something, but she was in the library getting tutoring," I said.

"Maria puts on airs, but she's ranked like fiftieth in our class, which isn't enough to stand out. Her uncle went to Princeton, but there's no way she's getting in without a major donation."

"Well, it's a good enough alibi. If she was there with Oscar, I doubt she was creeping around other people's computers. I'll cross her off the list for now, and revisit her if nobody else pans out, okay?" I said. "And it wasn't Josh, either."

I didn't bother mentioning that after today, I was done being her errand boy. If I happened to hear something about her flash drive, I'd clue her in, but the case no longer concerned me. With the deputies off my back, there was no reason for me to help her, and I hadn't forgotten how she'd tried to blackmail me. Dear Neighbor and I were through.

We made it home, and when we reached the spot between our houses, my seat belt flew off and I practically jumped out of the car.

"You're welcome!" Bridget yelled after me.

ANSWERS

I COOKED A CHICKEN POTPIE IN THE MICROWAVE AND SAT down with it at the table while my parents subjected me to the interrogation I'd been bracing for all day at school. They circled me like wolves.

"So you and Bridget spent the better part of last night and early morning texting each other questionable messages?" Mom asked.

"I think it's called 'sexting,'" said Dad. It was the worst sentence uttered in the history of my life.

"I didn't say anything in front of you guys before because I was embarrassed, but we explained everything to the deputies later."

Dad frowned. "I think that kind of 'conversing' is best kept private. I'm glad you're not going to be harassed by the sheriff's department anymore, but digital files are forever. You didn't send pictures, I hope?"

"No! God. No."

"Are you dating Bridget again?" asked Mom. "I thought you were still upset about Ellie. I mean, not that I think one is better than the other ..."

"Yeah, no, Bridget and I were just joking around ..." I squirmed in my seat, wishing the potpie would cool down so I could shovel it in my mouth. Actually, I should've shoveled it in anyway. Better to burn the roof of my mouth off and be rendered mute than deal with any more of this discussion.

Besides, *clearly* Ellie was better. How could there be any doubt? My mom's not one of those "No one's good enough for my baby boy" types, but Ellie was superior to Bridget both on paper and in reality. Did she really not see a difference between them?

"Speaking of Ellie, she called an hour ago."

Way to bury the lede, Dad. I bolted from my seat and reached for the landline.

"Finish your dinner first; she can wait," said Mom.

"Let him call her if he wants," said Dad. "It might be important."

"Did you ever figure out why she broke things off?" Mom asked.

It took me a second to realize she was addressing me and not just spouting theories to my dad.

"I think she's freaking out about college. I think she just needs time," I said, placing the receiver back on the hook. "Can I eat in my room?"

When I picked up the receiver, there was no dial tone. Odd. I was about to hang up when a voice said, "Charlie?"

"Yeah?"

"It's Ryder. Did the phone even ring? How'd you know I—"

"I was about to make a call," I said, mildly concerned. Ryder never called my house. "What's up?"

"I know you've been asking around about a flash drive," he said. "I'm saying this because we're friends, but I'm only going to say it once. You don't know what you're getting into, so get out before it becomes a problem." He never raised his voice. He didn't need to.

In some ways he was like Ellie. They could both be soft-spoken, which forced you to lean in, and it gave their words more impact than a shout.

I looked out the window at Bridget's house, as if I could find answers there. The whole thing had seemed suspicious from the start, but now my curiosity was piqued.

"What's the big deal?" I asked.

"The less you know, the better. It's not worth dragging yourself into, you know?"

"Can I call you back?" I said.

"I'm not at home. We'll talk tomorrow."

He hung up before I could respond. I'd already decided not to help Bridget anymore, but Ryder was a different story. Was this his roundabout way of asking for help, or did he genuinely want me to stop looking into the flash drive? What was really going on?

Nothing I could do at the moment except call Ellie back, so I put my questions aside.

I sat on the bedroom floor and leaned against my bed, the phone balanced between my shoulder and ear, as I'd done almost every night when Ellie and I had been dating.

My breath sped up as I dialed her number, because it was both familiar and terrifying to be calling her again. It felt like our future hinged on this conversation. I dialed slowly, holding each number down as long as I could, and listening to the robotic tones of each one. I took a deep breath and hit the final number.

"Sorry I wasn't there after choir, I had to go get Jonathan," Ellie said after picking up. I'd been vacillating between "Hey, babes" and "May I speak to Ellie, please?" so it was good she'd cut to the chase. Neither opening line would've set the right tone.

"That's okay. I'm glad you called," I said. Formality was painful, even more painful than fighting. Formality meant we were over, so we may as well be civil. But I didn't know how else to act. I had no visual cues to tell me her state of mind.

"Sure."

"So, um . . ."

"I know I owe you a better explanation. I just—let me close the door." She did so, and returned. "A week before we had coffee, a girl I've barely even talked to before saw me shopping at the mall and asked if I could hook her up with some snow for the holidays." She sounded far away.

"What?" I said, trying to draw her voice closer, scared she might fade to nothing.

"Yeah. I didn't know what she meant." I could tell this was hard for her to talk about—that maybe she was afraid her parents would hear, even with the door closed. She affected a dumb drawl. "I was all, 'Are ya goin' skiin'?' "

"What's 'snow'?" I asked, even though I had a pretty good idea.

"Cocaine." She attacked the Cs, then lowered her voice again. "She heard I was the girl to ask."

I was shocked. "What? Why?"

"I chalked it up to a misunderstanding at first, but then it happened again, a couple days later. Someone asked me to bring 'refreshments' to a party."

"Why would they think—"

"Because I was dating you. And you work for Ryder." Her voice solidified—hardened—and formed edges. "Apparently I have the hook-up, and I didn't even know it. So, what's fair-market price these days? Think I could get a discount?"

"Okay, okay." I nodded slowly, as though she could see me, or at least sense how seriously I was taking this. They say if you smile when making a sales call, the person on the other end will feel it in the tenor of your voice, so I nodded like my life depended on it. "Okay . . . I sometimes do favors for him, but it's not—it's not drugs. It's not what you think. It's the history classroom. I leave the window unlocked once a week."

"Why?"

I took a moment. "I've never asked."

"Sure. Why ask, as long as the money keeps coming in?" Her voice was soft again, but sarcastic, and it stung me like a cut lip squirted with pomegranate juice.

I swallowed. "Look. It didn't seem like a big deal. He's my oldest friend."

She exhaled, a brief snort. I could practically hear her rolling her eyes, and it drove me nuts. Everyone was happy to write off Ryder, because they didn't know him, but they were willing to *use* him when it suited their purposes. Even Ellie.

"Okay, remember when you got a parking pass junior year? And so did I? And so did all our friends?" I said.

She seemed perplexed by the subject change. "The parking lottery, yeah."

"Did you really think it was luck?"

"That's what a lottery is."

"There were only twenty-five passes available for juniors. Out of the whole school, you and I both got passes. And you didn't think that was strange?"

There was a pause. "You rigged the lottery?"

"I told you I'd take care of it, and I did. You were thrilled. You weren't asking too many questions then."

She gave a sound that was half laughter, half horror, like she couldn't decide if she should be impressed or concerned. "I can't believe you rigged the lottery."

"Ryder and I did it together. It was easy. We paid off the hall monitor who collected everyone's slips, and he paid off the dot-gov to read the names of our friends and yours and mine."

"You bribed the student council president?!"

"No, we paid off the VP, and Ryder 'delayed' the president from attending."

"Is that supposed to be better?"

"C'mon. You had to have known something was up, but you didn't say anything."

"Maybe," she conceded. "I guess I didn't want to know. And I didn't think it was a big deal—I mean, someone had to get those passes."

"Right," I said. "And if you'd ever spent time with Ryder, you'd know he's not like that. Yes, he gets high sometimes, but he's not a *dealer*. You'd get high, too, if you got beaten up every day freshman year. He's had a rough time at home, but he's a good guy."

"What he did for you in Little League was amazing," Ellie said carefully, "but that was a long time ago. I think you have to open your eyes to who he is *now*."

"He threw the bat for me," I said. "There's nothing else to say."

She didn't reply.

"Why didn't you tell me about the drugs?" I asked. "I could've explained all that to you."

"There were other things, too," she said quietly, reluctantly.

I hung on every word, nervous and sick.

"Like what?"

"When I met you, you played center forward—you were like this blur of light all over the field, assisting goals, taking shots. You were a leader."

"You dumped me because I got moved to fullback?" I said, incredulous.

"No, of course not!"

"Then what are you trying to say?"

"You were different. All of a sudden, it was like you wanted to *hurt* people—"

"It's a sport, Ellie. There's going to be contact."

"You used to play for sixty, eighty minutes . . . Now you're a hit man, in and out in five to kick people or shove them down."

"I'm just trying to help my team! I didn't *want* to be put on defense. It just happened, so I'm trying to make the most of it."

"It happened because you got more aggressive."

As the phone call had gone on, I'd been sliding inexorably toward the floor, until by this point I was basically lying down, a puddle of ooze, defeated. "Anything else?" I asked the ceiling.

"Both things made me scared for you. I got this feeling something terrible was going to happen, either with Ryder or with soccer. Like you were on the edge of something bad and you were going to get hurt, or you were going to hurt someone, and Jonathan—"

"What's this have to do with Jonathan?"

"He looks up to you. So much. And I didn't want him to see you this way, or have him be around drugs or—"

"I would never—"

"It just scared me, okay?"

"But you don't—you don't think I had anything to do with *West Side Story* Maria's overdose, do you?"

She didn't reply, which was worse than a straight-out accusation. At least you can defend yourself from those.

"I didn't . . . I swear to God I'm as much in the dark as anyone else is." My parents believed me unconditionally; why couldn't Ellie?

"I know. I think. I mean ..."

"I wish you'd told me all this so I could've fixed it, you know?"

The silence was so long, I had to make sure she was still there. "Ellie?"

"I wanted to, but I got the feeling you don't trust me anymore," she said, which broke whatever was left of my heart.

I dragged myself upright again and propped my back against the bed. "Did you really apply to Lambert, or was that just something you told me?"

"See? That's exactly what I'm talking about. You don't trust me. Your first instinct when you saw me with Fred was to accuse me of, like, cheating on you."

I took a deep breath, painfully aware that she hadn't answered my real question. "I miss you," I murmured. "You said you still care about me, too." She hadn't, I knew; she'd said she still "worried" about me, but it sounded better to use the word "care." "If I change all those things, do we have a shot?"

"But you *can't* change those things," she said. "You didn't think they were a problem. So if you change them, you'd only be doing it because I asked you to, not because you agree with me."

There was a clicking noise, and we both quieted.

"Charlie?"

It was Jonathan.

I exhaled. "What up, J-Dawg." Maybe it was kind of mean that I called him that. He was a scrawny sci-fi nerd in glasses, hardly gangsta. But he seemed to like it.

"Jonathan, hang up. We're having a private conversation," said Ellie.

"I haven't been listening. I just got on because I need to ask Charlie something."

"Go for it," I said. Any distraction would be better than the conversation Ellie and I had been having.

"Do you remember saying you were going to take me to *Blood of Mars* this Wednesday for the sneak preview? We saw the trailer over Thanksgiving? Do you remember saying that?"

"Sure," I said. "The only problem is, I don't have a car right now."

"Oh, maaaan," he said.

"I know," I said. "My thoughts exactly." I waited a beat, as if the idea had just occurred to me. "Maybe Ellie could take us. If she's feeling generous."

Ellie laughed, a nice laugh, not a sarcastic one, and it felt like sparkling water being poured down my throat, bubbly and cleansing. "Subtle."

"Ugh, I don't want to go with Ellie. She hates sci-fi," said Jonathan.

"I know, but I don't think we have any other options. If you want to see it before everyone else, I mean."

This was torture for him. If he didn't see it the first possible night, he may as well not see it at all. It'd be ruined; the other kids or the Internet would spoil it for him. He must've read my mind because he nearly burst my eardrum. "Pleeeeease, Ellie?"

"Pleeeeease?" I echoed.

"Oh my God, fine, but only if you stop whining. Both of you."

"Pick me up at seven?" I said quickly, before she could change her mind. "I'll buy the tickets. See you Wednesday night."

Maybe I'd only succeeded in prolonging the inevitable. But for now, that was enough.

We hung up and I pulled my shoe box of Ellie memorabilia out from under the bed and turned it upside down, shaking the contents onto the floor. There were a bunch of folded, handwritten notes on her signature stationery, which was dark blue, like her Homecoming dress. She used to write in white pen—occasionally backwards, if she had snoops breathing over her shoulder, so I'd had to use a mirror to read those.

A few loose photographs and seven thick Post-it pads were mixed in with the notes. I picked up one of the Post-it pads and flipped through it. Ellie liked to draw these elaborate animated flip-book cartoons for me when she was bored in class. Sometimes she'd re-create me on the soccer field, or draw us kissing, or draw herself at Wahoo's Fish Taco, gobbling up tacos like Pac-Man. She loved California cuisine; couldn't get enough of Asian fusion and Cobb salads and tacos and sushi.

For our first date, at her request, I'd taken her to Wahoo's Fish Taco.

I'd been wolfing my food down, but she'd kept rotating her plate, taking a bite from each section of rice, guacamole, and taco, and when I asked her why, she said she was trying to plan it so she ended with a piece of avocado. She'd decided in advance what she

73

wanted the last bite to be; she liked to end her meal on just the right note.

I ate that way now. Sometimes. Just because it reminded me of her.

She wasn't my alcohol; she never had been. She was my water, the thing I'd been thirsting for, the thing that would save me.

But how do you hold on to water? It never stops moving. It flows away, it changes shape, it returns to its source.

It evaporates.

IN THE BACK OF THE BUS

THE NEXT DAY, TUESDAY, I WONDERED IF BRIDGET WAS RIGHT.
That I didn't move fast enough, hadn't moved fast enough with
Ellie. But we'd talked about it—a lot. Neither of us wanted empty
sex, or stressful sex, or covert, rushed sex in a car or on the couch
while her parents and brother were out. We didn't want all the
time we'd spent together, all the hours we'd talked on the phone, to
end up being nothing more than a prelude to Getting It On. I was
afraid if we did it, the whole relationship would become about sex,
the way it had with Bridget and me.

Bridget was the kind of girl you dated because everyone else
seemed to want her. I'd loved the idea of her, and I'd loved having
a girlfriend, but I was never *in* love with her. She was pushy and
abrasive, and she was always pointing out my supposed flaws. We
went parking at Devil's Punchbowl hiking preserve on our first
date, and when I walked her to her door, she made fun of me for
not getting to second base. I didn't think it was okay to just go
ahead and grab a girl's tits. I figured you had to build up to it. She
decided I needed coaching and I was a willing student, but when
she showed me the condom in her purse a few weeks later, I didn't

feel excited; I felt dread. We'd barely been together a month. I didn't want to have sex with someone I wasn't in love with, at least, not for my first time, so I told her no thanks, and she was insulted, so she broke up with me.

When Ellie moved here, I knew instantly what I'd been missing. We moved slowly, but that was hotter because instead of feeling rushed, like I had with Bridget, I felt like Ellie and I were testing boundaries *together*. I just wanted her to be happy and relaxed, and I didn't care if sex happened in a month or a year.

Bridget didn't think I was aggressive enough, and Ellie thought I was too aggressive (at least, on the soccer field). How the hell was someone both too much and not enough?

Like a cat with burrs on its back, I tried to shake my dark musings loose, but some of them stuck. If we'd had sex, would Ellie still have broken up with me? Or would we have been tied together in some stronger way that was more difficult to undo?

At breakfast, my dad shoveled in his Shredded Wheat like he was halfway out the door, so I asked quickly, "Did the sheriff's department call with an ETA about when I can get Amelia back?"

"Not until Thursday. And I can't drive you this morning because I'm already late for a faculty meeting. Sorry."

Maybe this makes me sound like I was still drunk, but for the first time since my car had been impounded, it dawned on me what the situation really meant.

It meant—oh Jesus God—I had to take the bus.

I hadn't ridden the bus to school in two years. I wasn't even sure where it picked people up. Squinting in the January sunlight, I looked in both directions and saw a couple of underclassmen hunched over their smartphones across the street and down a block.

I adjusted my backpack and strolled over to wait in line, trying to look like I didn't care that I was a senior waiting for the goddamn yellow-and-black. The two clogged pores were playing Guttersnipes Versus Woodpeckers, but then one of them looked up and saw me.

"Charlie Dixon?" he nudged his friend. "That's—are you Charlie Dixon?"

Since they'd initiated the conversation, it was okay to reply. "I also answer to Dix, Chazz, or Chuckles. Actually, I don't. What do you want?"

"You're on the soccer team."

The second clogged pore looked up now. "No way."

The first guy went into a frenzy of elbow nudges. "I told you he lived on our block." He turned back to me. "I saw you wipe out that guy from Agua Dulce last fall. Red card in the fourth minute. Suh-weet."

It was disconcerting that what they remembered from the game was me fouling Steve, not me scoring or assisting or defending the box, but hey—I happened to be the player who slid cleats-first into opponents to steal the ball. Someone had to be, right?

"Who are you with?" I asked, trying to change the subject.

"Orchestra. Are you gonna nail him like that again on Friday?" the second frosh asked.

"Haven't decided," I said. Maybe I'd rather be remembered for something else. It was a little too much philosophizing for 7:15 in the morning. "You guys play?"

"Hellz yeah. We have a game in the street every Thursday night," the first guy said. "You should come."

His buddy shoved him. "He has *real* practice every night, 'tard."

"It's cool," I said. "Hey, is that today's issue?"

"Yeah."

"How'd you get a copy already?" I asked.

The *Palm Valley High Recorder* came out on Tuesdays, with issues appearing in stacks outside the principal's office, cafeteria, and journalism room. They shouldn't be available outside school yet, but this one had today's date on it.

"My sister's the coeditor. She brought one home last night."

"Can I take a look at it?" I said.

He was delighted, practically threw it at me. "Yeah, here, keep it."

The bus pulled up and I motioned for the little dudes to go ahead in front of me. It was friggin' embarrassing climbing up the steps inside the bus, like I was returning to childhood. I half expected Mom to appear on the sidewalk outside the house, waving good-bye in exaggerated motions or racing after the bus to hand me my brown-bag lunch with a smiley face drawn on it.

I strolled to the back of the bus, doing my best to ignore the rows of curious eyes and excited murmurs following me. The clogged pores had already spread the word that Charlie Dixon, local soccer antihero, was inexplicably gracing them with his presence this morning.

"I saved a spot for you," one of them chimed from the very last seat.

"Move," I said, pointing to a spot in front. I wanted the back seat to myself, so I could have privacy while reading the school paper.

I settled in and flipped straight to the last page—the classifieds and gossip section. Not everyone's parents let them use Facebook, so if you wanted to get a message out schoolwide, establish an introduction to an underclassman, or make romantic intentions known, the newspaper was still the best way to do it.

A little over a year ago, Ellie had signaled her interest in these pages. I still had the scrap, faded and yellowing, in my shoe box of Ellie stuff. It read, "Which East Coast transplant doesn't want to be too Forward about her crush?" At the time, junior year, I was center forward, and everyone knew it.

I still found it strange that she'd aligned herself with girls' choir when she moved here. A lot of groups in school wanted to claim her, but she belonged nowhere—and everywhere. The chekhovs came closest, at first, until she explained she wasn't reading Chekhov's stories or plays for anyone but herself. Not for a teacher, not for a grade. She told me once the reason she liked his work was because she could never tell if she'd understood it. Finding out if she had or hadn't by discussing it with other people seemed vulgar to her; it would've sapped all the joy out of it.

Maria Posey took one look at Ellie, saw she was worth knowing, and invited her to be a songbird. Ellie was just an okay singer—which suited Maria fine. That meant she wouldn't be competition.

The day I saw Ellie's message to me in the paper, I made it a point to say hi to her in no-man's-land before the game. I'd had my eye on her for ages but acted like my interest was brand-new. I asked what she was doing after the match, and she said she was hoping I would ask, and the rest is too happy and painful to go into.

Today's issue was the first since our breakup and I guess I thought there might be a mention to close it out, a hidden message, *something* from or about her.

I skimmed the whole page, fighting off the pounding headache that dehydration, dead alcohol, and reading on a bouncing bus induced, and that's when I saw it. The final message. They were listed in order received, so it must have been added right before deadline last night.

"To ChD. If you find it, don't give it to her. I'll pay more. IM 10 2nite."

The flash drive again!

Ryder's warning came back to me. I'd been so caught up in my Ellie call last night I'd forgotten about the conversation that preceded it.

I read the message three more times, my heart racing. The person who'd written it was willing to pay for the drive. If I managed to find it, there were apparently several interested parties.

I dug through my backpack for Bridget's list of suspects and leaned over to the clogged pores in the seat ahead. "You know this kid Danny? Who's he run with?"

They looked at each other, decided it was safe to tell me, and nodded. "He's with the art kids—charcoal sketches, that kind of thing."

"Who do I need to see? Is Jake still in charge?"

They nodded again.

"I'll square things with Jake, but in the meantime, can you find Danny this morning and tell him I want a word? Tell him to meet me at the water fountain outside the art room after first period."

"Okay," the first clogged pore said.

"So what do we get for facilitating this?" the second clogged pore said.

I laughed. "You get me not kicking your ass."

They looked nervous for a second, so I rolled my eyes. "What do you think is fair payment?"

"At the soccer game on Friday, we might have dates . . ."

"Uh-huh," I said dryly.

"If we come up to you, act like we're pals. And maybe see that we have good seats."

Having had little to no truck with them before today, I understood within five minutes why it was so tempting to beat the crap out of freshmen; but I also had to admire their style. "Sure, fine. What are your names?"

They told me and I promptly forgot, but that was okay because I was good with faces. I'd put on a nice show for their supposed girlfriends and maybe pay for a couple of hot dogs and Cokes to be sent over to their section.

I dismissed my new foot soldiers.

I couldn't believe it was only Tuesday morning, only forty-eight hours since *West Side Story* Maria had been dumped at the hospital. She should've been heading to school right now with the rest of us. She should've been pissing off the other songbirds by practicing her concert solo in the hallway. She should've been looking all around with those big, sad eyes of hers and taking in the same weary world as me.

As head of the art kids, Jake controlled who interacted with his charges. Art boys were notoriously bullied by upperclassmen, more so than the rest of the groups combined, so Jack was overprotective.

If I'd approached Danny out of nowhere to question or accuse him, it'd be like declaring war on every potter, jeweler, painter, sketcher, and wind chimer at school. Worse, they had an alliance with the drama kids, and you did *not* want to make enemies of the drama kids. Not because they were scary; they were just . . . dramatic. They would band together, write original arias and skits about you, and corner you in the hallway or cafeteria to publicly shame you for what you'd done. Sometimes it went on for *days*.

Since the library was no-man's-land, a lot of romances originated there. If you couldn't or didn't want to wait for a formal introduction, you could meet on the sly in the stacks, but it was all on the down low and could easily backfire.

I prided myself on my social mobility. I was welcome with the beckhams, a few other sports that overlapped, the songbirds (because of Ellie), and several people in my neighborhood (Bridget, plus now the clogged pores from this morning). I had *some* unofficial clout with the journos because of my dad's job, and his occasional columnist work for the *Palm Valley Register*. He'd given my classmates a tour of the newspaper office last year. That might've been one of the reasons Bridget had asked me for help; it was quicker for me to interview the people on her list because I didn't have to schedule as many meetings as the one I was about to.

I hovered outside the art classroom, waiting for Jake to show and watching the clock. I took out Bridget's list of names again and studied it. Josh was crossed off definitively, but before I could cross off Maria Posey, I had to make sure that one of the other ID numbers matched Oscar, her tutor. It did. Seemed she'd been straight with me. I crossed her off and shoved the list away in time to see Jake approach. He was wearing overalls and a Nine Inch Nails T-shirt, both dotted with paint.

"Charlie." He nodded shortly.

"Jake," I replied.

"The bell's imminent."

"I know. Sorry to keep this last-minute, but I need to speak with your boy Danny after first period, at the water fountain. Nothing serious, just getting data for a friend about an incident in no-man's-land Friday morning."

"What makes you think Danny has anything to do with whatever's going on?"

"I've been told he might have seen someone swipe a flash drive that didn't belong to them. I'm looking at Danny as a witness, not a suspect, and I'll treat him accordingly."

Jake's expression remained blank. *Impress me, soccer boy.*

"I also told two freshmen to make the intro for me, on the bus this morning," I added.

That seemed to do the trick. "So he won't be ambushed?"

"No, he'll be expecting it."

Jake nodded again. The bell rang. I looked at him for final confirmation.

"I'm going to allow it," said Jake. "But next time give me twenty-four hours' notice. And I might drop by."

We shook hands and went our separate ways.

Danny was a quivering wreck at our meet-and-greet. I think my minions from the bus told him I was a bruiser or something. He looked more like a seventh grader than a freshman, and he reminded me of Ellie's brother, who actually *was* a seventh grader. I tried to put Danny's mind at ease.

"Hi. Thanks for agreeing to this. I'm Charlie."

"I know."

"Look, I just want to know if you saw anything suspicious in the library, second period, on Friday. A friend of mine had a flash drive stolen."

"Who's your friend?"

"Bridget Flannery."

His face got pink. Jesus, he was blushing.

"You know who that is?" I said.

He nodded, apparently mute with lust. I was glad his sketchbook was in front of his crotch.

"She was sitting at the computer near the far left window," I said. "Where were you sitting? Did you see anything?"

"Is she your girlfriend?" Danny asked. He seemed to be fundamentally confused about the order and purpose of a Q & A.

"She lives next door to me," I replied, with all the patience I could muster. "Did you see anything?"

"She lives next door to you?" he sputtered. "Ohhhh my God."

"Yes, that's how our real estate agent listed the house. Bridget-Adjacent Property."

"Can you see in her window?"

"I'm gonna pretend you didn't ask me that, *Danny*." Maria Posey was so right; names could be used as insults all day long, and there was no shortage of targets at this school.

"I just—"

"Stop dribbling down your shirt and answer the question. Did you see anyone take a flash drive from that or any other computer at the end of second period?"

"No." Danny shifted from one foot to the other. "But—"

My patience careened downhill like an out-of-control skateboard about to crash. "But what?"

"I don't want to get anyone in trouble..."

"You're gonna be the one in trouble if you don't answer me."

"It's just . . . I was at the library second period last Friday, but Bridget wasn't."

I stared at him. "*Bridget* wasn't there?"

"No."

"And you're sure we're talking about the same Bridget?"

He placed his sketchbook under his armpit and made the universal sign for "hourglass curves" with his hands. I was embarrassed on his behalf and pushed his hands away, just when Jake walked up, of course.

"Everything cool here?" Jake demanded, moving protectively in front of Danny.

I leaned around him to address Danny. "Your perv-in-training was about to sketch me a picture."

Danny opened his sketchpad and pressed it flat against the wall. He rapidly drew a picture of a girl's face with his charcoal.

"If she'd been there, I would've noticed," he said.

"I believe you," I said. The likeness was uncanny. I half expected the drawing to come to life and make an obscene gesture at us with its tongue.

I tore the picture out of Danny's sketchpad, handed the pad back to him, and said, "I might need you for a favor later. Check in by the fountain again tomorrow."

"Will Bridget be there?" he asked eagerly.

"Sure," I said, but it was a lie.

"You've been lying to me."

"Well, hello to you, too, grouchy," Bridget said, twirling the combination on her lock. "School bus not what it used to be?"

"I didn't see you offering to give me a ride," I snarled. "Thanks, neighbor."

She was incredulous. "If you'd been nicer to me last night, maybe I would have."

"Nicer, like hands-on? Never gonna happen again. Now, give me a copy of your schedule."

She opened her locker, but I slammed it shut and leaned against it, blocking her access.

Her eyes narrowed. "Why?"

"I want to know where I can find you at all times."

"Wow, Dix, I'm super-flattered, but—" She flicked her head to the side.

"You want me to move? You want your books for third period? Hand over your schedule."

She pulled out her iPhone, which was off, and mimed tapping out an e-mail. "Dear Ellie, wass up girlfriend? Charlie tastes like cheap whiskey and despair, how could you ever let him go? And 'send.'"

"Thank you, school board, for jamming our cell phones," I said. "As long as we're on campus you have no power over me."

"Because it would be so much trouble to send those texts when I go out to lunch."

"I erased the texts."

She'd forgotten; you could tell. Her voice changed to false confidence. "I . . . kept backups. I learned after losing my flash drive."

"I don't believe you. So I'm off the 'case' unless you come clean with me."

She sighed and opened her Trapper Keeper, where her schedule was taped to the inside flap. I scanned it quickly, shaking my head with disgust.

"You don't even *have* study hall second period."

"Most of the time, no," she admitted. She rifled through a couple of folders until she found a little slip of paper, which she flashed in front of my eyes for about a millisecond. "A pass from the guidance counselor. Special circs."

"How come your freshman stalker doesn't remember seeing you?"

"I wore my glasses that day. I'd pulled an all-nighter."

"You have an answer for everything. Guess I'm not asking my questions quickly enough."

I stepped aside and she opened her locker to get her books. A folded piece of notebook paper fluttered out from the vent. "What's that?" I said suspiciously.

Bridget bent over to get it. Traffic in the hallway screeched to a halt.

She slowly straightened up, cupped her hand around the piece of paper, and read it. The contents made her face blanch.

"What's it say?" I asked.

She slapped the note against my chest. "Still think I'm lying to you?"

I peeled the note out of her fingers and read it aloud. " 'I know someone who has something of yours. What's the information worth to you? Write a number on the back of this paper and Dix will give it to me.' "

My expression must have changed, because suddenly Bridget was in my face.

"You know who it's from, don't you?" she demanded. "If you know, you better tell me."

"I'll take care of it." I pocketed the note and got the hell out of there.

I'd recognize Ellie's handwriting anywhere, even if it hadn't been on dark blue stationery, written in white pen.

THE MOBILE ESTATES

AT LUNCH I COULD BARELY CONCENTRATE ON MY MEETING with Ryder.

He asked if we could walk back to his place for leftover pasta. I said I wasn't hungry so it didn't matter to me. We set off down the sidewalk, and he lit a cigarette the second we stepped off campus.

"Rough about Ellie," he said.

I nodded thanks. Rougher now that she was apparently shaking down Bridget for cash. If she'd needed money, why hadn't she come to me?

"Dumping you over Christmas break? *Damn.*"

"I know. I drank a gallon of eggnog at my cousin's." *And wine. And whiskey.*

"You had her longer than anyone thought you would, though," he said with a laugh, punching me lightly in the shoulder, and I had to laugh, too. I don't know why. That's how it was with Ryder. He could say anything, but instead of being offended, you saw the awful truth of his words and they struck you as genuinely funny. Besides, hadn't I spent the last eight months thinking the same thing?

He offered me a drag of his cigarette. I took a puff, handed it back, and shoved my hands in my pockets without response.

"Freaking songbirds, right?" he said after a while.

"What?"

"I saw you with Bridget in the hall," Ryder continued. "Are you rebounding? I don't think it counts if you just bounce between the same two." He cocked his head to the side, considering. "Unless of course, they're in the same bed . . ." He grinned.

I rolled my eyes. "No, man, Bridget's a pain in the ass. We're just handcuffed together in hell."

"I guess who you choose depends on if you're in the mood for a deficit or a surplus," he said.

I knew what he meant. Ellie was svelte; Bridget was . . . an hourglass motion in a hornball art kid's hands. They were both pretty, so personality trumped all. "She's got nothing on Ellie," I said.

"Maria Posey called me a cylon the other day. I don't even know what that shit means. Chicks around here need subtitles."

"You're with *Sound of Music* Maria?" I said with surprise. They hadn't *seemed* together, but why else would he have been at her party?

" 'With' is a strong word. 'Tormented by,' maybe."

"If you're a cylon, it means you're a robot who looks like a human," I explained. "It's from *Battlestar Galactica*."

"Like, 'I-am-a-robot'?" he said robotically.

"No, they look and sound exactly like people. I guess she meant you're acting inhuman, or cold, or something?" Weird that Posey, of all people, would have nerdish leanings.

"I always forget you're into comics."

"It's a TV—never mind. What was the context?"

"I wouldn't help her out with something."

I laughed. "I wouldn't worry about it. Posey's kind of hyperbolic."

Ryder raised his eyebrows in agreement and flicked his cigarette to the pavement.

We were passing the old baseball diamond, and just by looking out there at the empty grass I could conjure up that sense of liberation and chaos and pure joy I'd experienced when Ryder threw the bat for me.

Despite the stench of cigarettes that clung to his clothes and the restless look in his eyes, it was impossible for me to separate the Ryder of today from the Ryder of Little League.

We reached Mobile Estates, the cruelest euphemism in the world, even worse than Inland Empire. Both terms slapped you in the face about how crappy things were and then told you to smile about it. If trailer parks were "estates" and sprawling, bankrupt counties with no future were "empires," then "faking it and faking it hard" applied to society as a whole, not just Palm Valley High School. What a dismal revelation.

Did that mean I had to pretend to be a jock the rest of my life?

Ryder halted abruptly, so I did likewise. "Did you have a chance to think about what I said yesterday?" His tone had changed. We were being serious now.

"Maybe if I had more information . . ."

"So me asking you to back off isn't enough?" Ryder said.

He didn't wait for me to respond, just started walking again as though the matter were settled.

We entered his family's trailer and made ourselves comfortable at the table.

Ryder's older brother, Griffin, was in the other room, playing the latest Grand Theft Auto derivative. Muffled explosions, screams, and gunfire filtered out from under the door. Griffin had dropped out of school to work construction, but I don't think it took.

I was glad Griffin was in the other room. He always made me nervous.

Before we moved to Palm Valley, Ryder's mom used to teach home ec at Palm Valley High and Ryder's dad worked night security at one of the local military suppliers.

His dad got caught photocopying plans for the new vehicle barrier system, intending to sell them to a private contractor. It wasn't easy to find another job after that, particularly in the "Aerospace Capital of America," where discretion is the first requirement. And when Ryder's mom was fired from teaching, thanks to Fresh Start, her husband had already been out of work for over a year.

Their house got foreclosed on, and Ryder's mom took a position working the front desk at the rental office for Mobile Estates. The position came with a place to live but almost nothing to live *on*. A longtime tenant harassed her at work on a daily basis. Ryder's dad took care of the situation, leading to an assault charge; after a brief stint behind bars he was picked up again for fencing stolen auto parts at a chop shop.

Now Ryder's mom was in rehab for painkillers, and Ryder's dad was "vacationing" in North Lancaster prison; visiting hours were noon to five every other Saturday. My parents had offered to drive Ryder over there on a number of occasions, but he always declined. I don't think he'd seen the old man in years.

Ryder never blamed me for his family's problems, but Griffin was a different story. The day after my bike was tampered with and destroyed, Griffin asked where my wheels were, and when I told him what had happened, he smiled.

I hoped Ryder and I would be in, out, and done with lunch before Griffin saw fit to emerge from his cave.

Ryder took a fat money clip out of his back pocket and counted out four twenties. Eighty dollars, twice what he normally paid. Was I being bought off to forget about the flash drive?

"What's this for?" I said.

"I might need the window unlocked again on Wednesday. I trust you; I know you're good for it. I'll let you know, but either way you can keep it, just to be on standby."

I couldn't argue with that logic. "Is that going to be a thing from now on, twice a week?"

"Maybe, maybe not."

"Can I ask what you need it unlocked for?"

"I don't know. Can you?" he said.

I played along. "What do you need it unlocked for?"

"Sure you want to know? Could make you an accessory."

"Okay, *Criminal Minds*, I've been warned."

"Mr. Donovan keeps the pop quiz schedule and practice exams in his drawer. I crawl in the window, copy everything down, replace the sheets, and sell the intel."

I shook my head, impressed. *Of course.* Mr. Donovan wasn't some kind of *Stand and Deliver* svengali; he was the "best teacher at the school" because people knew about the tests in advance, and what would be on them. Mom would have a coronary if she found out.

"That's how I got hooked up with Maria Posey. Sometimes she pays, sometimes she . . . pays in other ways." He didn't need to wink to get the point across, so he didn't.

He went to the fridge, scooped out some leftovers onto a paper plate, and offered them to me. I shook my head.

"No thanks."

Ryder shrugged and grabbed a warm beer from a case on the floor, tossed it to me, and cracked one for himself.

I opened my liquid lunch. "What's the deal with *West Side Story* Maria?" I asked.

"They should just call her Salvador."

I laughed. "That's what I said. Any idea how she overdosed?"

"Yeah. Some people can't handle a party." Ryder shook his head ruefully.

"Were a lot of people doing LSD, or just her?" Bridget's words from Sunday night floated back to me, but not clearly; more like I remembered them from someone else's dream in which I was a bit player. *It's not that kind of party*, she'd said, lowering my flask out of sight.

"Some of the girls wanted to unwind after the stress of competition. But no one else overdosed, so it's tough to say."

"I saw her in the kitchen before it happened," I said.

"She was cute. *Is* cute. Posey would have my ass if she knew I said that. The Marias *hate* each other."

"Why?"

"There can only be one soloist in choir, right? It's right there in the name. But anyway, the reason I wanted to talk . . ."

"Any idea who dropped her at the ER? 'Cause they really wanted it to look like me."

"I heard about that. Yeah, I heard about that." He glanced toward the other room, where Griffin was, and lowered his voice. "We can talk about that later, but lunch period's almost over, so—"

"You said you had a way for me to make some real cash?" I said, taking a swig of my beer. I wasn't sure it would help my headache, but it couldn't make it worse. Liquor was foul, but watered-down Miller Lite barely registered with me anymore. It practically tasted like water, just enough to remind me it wasn't; I'd spend the next hour sideways, wishing I were on the other side.

Ryder knocked his can into mine and got down to business. "Yeah. So. The soccer game on Friday." He glanced toward the other room again. "Are you going to foul Agua Dulce?"

"That's the question of the day."

"Who else asked you that?" he said sharply.

"No one," I said, taken aback. "Just two clogged pores at the bus stop."

"And what'd you tell them?"

"That I have to see how it goes. Contrary to popular opinion, I don't actually plan when and how I'm going to foul someone. I still *play the game*. Fouling might be part of a strategy, but if there's a better way for me to get the ball, I do that instead."

"There's five hundred bucks with your name on it if you do what you normally do."

"And what do I normally do, exactly?" I said, teeth gritted.

"Foul the crap out of Steve as quickly as possible. Preferably when he's about to score."

"When he's about to score," I repeated.

"Yeah, just foul him like you normally do."

"But it won't be normal if I'm doing it because you told me to." I was reminded of Ellie's words to me on the phone last night. *"But you can't change those things,"* she'd said. *"You didn't think they were a problem. So if you change them, you'd only be doing it because I asked you to, not because you agree with me."*

"Pretend we never had this conversation, but know that if you do what you normally do, you'll be five hundred bucks richer," Ryder said simply.

I really wished I were still center forward instead of fullback. Then maybe Ryder would pay me to hit the back of the net, something I'd *want* to do. Winning should be what I normally do, not maiming.

"You want me to throw the game," I said slowly.

He made a motion like "lower your voice."

"Don't you?" I said, quieter.

"No, no, I just—"

"Foul him *when he's about to score?* After he's had a first touch, gearing up to strike, so he'll get a penalty kick."

He snorted. "You're overthinking things, man."

I folded my arms, certain I had his scheme pegged. "Steve's got the best PK conversion stats in LA County. If I give him a penalty kick, I'm *giving him* a score."

Ryder didn't say anything.

"Can't do it," I said. "If I'd decided to foul him on my own, in the heat of the game, that would be one thing, but asking me to deliberately lose a match? I have my faults, but that's not me."

Ryder finished his beer and crushed the can in his fist. "Okay, okay! Sorry I asked. I thought you'd be cool with it."

"That's what you think of me? That I don't care about the team, I don't care about our record? That I'd sell the guys out?"

He raised an eyebrow. "You didn't care about the lottery for junior parking spaces."

"Me having a damn parking space junior year is not the same thing as screwing up people's *scholarships*," I said, mostly because he had a point. Hadn't I used the exact same argument on Ellie?

All right, so I hadn't been a model student before, and maybe he was right in thinking my ethics were flexible. But it bothered me nonetheless. "College recruiters are going to be there. Maybe they're not looking at me, but they might pick Patrick or Delinksy. But not if Steve's scoring left and right! I can't do that to those guys."

Ryder's eyes were cold black pools. "Then don't show up, if you're such a team player all of a sudden," he said. "Just take the game off."

I wiped a tense hand down my face. "Oh, God. You bet against us, didn't you?"

"A thousand," said Ryder quietly. "It could pay off triple." He glanced around the trailer, at the filth coating every surface, the empty beer cans on the floor, and the stained mugs filled with cigarette butts and moldy coffee. "Thought I could skip town."

We stared at each other. *Shit.*

The sounds of gunfire and chaos in the other room abruptly stopped. "Yo, baby b," Griffin's hoarse voice called from behind the door. "We need your expertise."

"Where's he been all day?" another voice wanted to know.

"He went to school this morning," Griffin responded. Both voices erupted into high-pitched, hysterical laughter.

"Duty calls," Ryder said, a bitter edge to his voice. He stood up and offered me his hand. "Are we on the same page for all this, or what?"

I ignored his hand. Did "same page" mean forgetting about the flash drive, or did "same page" mean fouling Steve for cash? Did "same page" mean leaving the history window unlocked again on Wednesday? Had we agreed to something, and I'd been too buzzed to realize it?

"Aren't you coming?" I said, heading to the door.

"No, Charlie," he said in a tired voice, as though I were kind of slow, "I'm not going back to school today." He tapped his nose. "The nose knows."

There was a vibe in the air I didn't like. I just wanted to be back on the sidewalk, away from the trailer homes and out in the fresh air, away from my friend and all the ways our paths had separated since Little League.

Griffin appeared in the doorway. His hair was greasy, his face pockmarked, and he'd developed a bit of a sag around his belly since I'd seen him last. He'd scared the hell out of me when we were kids. He once pinned me down and made me drink an entire bottle of Seagram's Jamaican Me Happy.

Maybe I was never meant to like alcohol but always meant to drink it anyway. Maybe I wasn't into the high, I was into the familiarity.

Griffin clamped a hand on Ryder's shoulder and tucked a container of orange Tic Tacs into Ryder's shirt pocket, patting it protectively. He looked straight at me and chuckled, showing off a rotten tooth.

"Go get 'em, killer," Griffin said. I didn't know what he meant, but something about the words bothered me. It was just a feeling I had, that something was horribly wrong. And on the walk back to school I realized what it was.

He'd been wearing a Flynn Scientific baseball cap, exactly like the one worn by the driver of my car on the hospital security tape.

WHEN RYDER THREW
THE BAT

SIXTH GRADE. SUMMERTIME IN A NEW TOWN. NO SCHOOL, no homework, no responsibilities. It should have been a carefree couple of months, a chance for me to meet my classmates outside of school and show up at homeroom on the first day with an entire team of built-in friends. Mom signed me up for baseball the moment we moved to Palm Valley; we just made the cutoff date.

It was a good plan in theory, except for my all-encompassing fear of the Little League coach, Coach Tierson (a.k.a. Tears You One). He wasn't just a big guy; he was a red-faced spittle shooter, who, as far as I could tell, hated children. He was like a snapping bulldog on a leash, so close to throttling you that if it weren't for the choke chain of potential lawsuits, you'd be in pieces scattered all over the field.

My first mistake was showing up in a clean uniform the first day of practice. Everybody else on the team had broken theirs in; their pants and jerseys were smudged with dirt, grass stains, even dots of blood. Their gloves were dark with sweat marks. Their cleats were clogged with mud. I was sparkling. I looked like I'd stepped out of a commercial for Tide laundry detergent, and this immediately earned me Coach's ire. He thought I was soft. My shoes were new, from the Sports Chalet in town, and my glove still had the tag attached. Coach took one look at me and introduced me as the new kid all the way from New Mexico who was afraid to get down in the muck. *I guess you think we look dirty. Not used to the dirt, kid? Fifty push-ups, let me hear you count 'em, kiss the dirt, kiss the dirt.*

My second mistake was being my mother's son. Coach Tierson used to teach social studies at Palm Valley High. Well, now he had to reapply for the position against cheaper, nonunion hires, and it wasn't looking good for the ol' man. It was the only time I remembered being happy about a stranger's misfortune. The schadenfreude went down like a cherry Slurpee: it wired me up and left my brain tingly. Another drink that does nothing but make you thirsty. What is sugar, after all, but kids' booze?

My third mistake was telling everyone my granddad worked at Lockheed Martin, and how Lockheed was the name of Shadowcat's dragon in *X-Men*, and wasn't that swell? (To soothe the pain of moving, my father had bequeathed to me his entire comic book collection from the 1970s and 1980s.) This was a piece of trivia I thought the other boys might appreciate. Wasn't I clever, integrating a fun fact of Palm Valley with a fun fact about superheroes? What it got me was blank looks and a "nerd" brand.

I decided I'd better shut that part of myself down, quick. All of it. Everything I liked, everything that made me *me* was to be suppressed, ignored, and denied, until I could no longer remember what it was I'd been hiding. I'd be a jock. I'd be the quiet but effective type who said all he needed to say on the field via his baseball prowess.

In short, I'd be like Ryder.

Ryder was our star, the best hitter, runner, fielder, and thrower. His eyes were quick and bright, he was always accurately predicting where the ball would land, and he could catch anything: grounders, pop-ups, line drives, fly balls.

I was a good hitter, but I always threw my bat. I couldn't help it; it was like this trajectory my arms were on, and there was no way off the track once I started on it.

It was inevitable.

I could tell myself all morning, "Don't throw the bat"—I could be thinking it even as I stood at the plate—but it made no difference. I'd swing wide and connect with the ball, feel the tremors up and down my arms, the bat vibrating so hard it stung my palms, and I'd let go, the bat flying away and smashing into the chain-link fence. I'd be off and running toward first before any of it registered, until I could hear a faint din growing louder and louder like a train coming out of a tunnel, and then I'd realize it was a full-on meltdown from Coach Tierson. "Dixon! What have I told you about throwing your bat? Get back here and pick it up!"

Confused, I'd halt three-quarters of the way to first base, turn around, and look at Coach. He'd throw his glove onto the grass, scattering dust and grit, and start toward me. The urge to flee would nearly overwhelm me; *It's not worth it, Charlie*, I'd think, *just get out of here* . . . I didn't even know how to find my new house from the field, though. If I'd taken off running, I'd be lost. I was stranded out there, helpless, until Mom came to pick me up. Besides, it was too late to run; I was frozen in place, dumbfounded and perplexed about what I'd done wrong, and he was a red-faced blubbery flubber storming toward me.

Day after day, the same words flung like shit against a wall, and I was the wall. I was worthless, a pussy, a fucking pussy, was I going to cry like a pussy? Did I need to practice with a NERF? Did he have to duct tape my hands to the bat so I wouldn't throw it?

When I told Ellie a shortened version of the story, the put-downs were the part she found most infuriating. "Why does every man think the absolute worst insult he can sling is to call someone a girl? And now all those boys think so, too. Asshole."

I just knew I was terrified of him.

We always had to hustle, too. *Don't lose that hustle; let me see you hustle; who's got the best hustle; hustle, infield; hustle, outfield; move it, move it! Ryder's got the right idea, if only I had a team full of Ryders maybe we woulda won last night against Pacoima.*

I thought about telling Dad. Every night at dinner, when he'd ask how practice was going and if I'd made any friends, I'd feel a lump form in my throat, poured there like concrete and hardened into a ball so I couldn't talk. I was afraid what Coach Tierson said about me was true, and that my dad would immediately see it. I was soft. Useless. A loser who couldn't hustle.

Deep down I wondered if Dad was soft, too; if that's where I'd gotten it from.

Besides, if I told my parents, it would only get worse. If they confronted Tierson but kept me enrolled in Little League, he would take it out on me even more. If they confronted Tierson and pulled me *out* of Little League, the whole team would know I'd squealed and I'd be a laughingstock for not being tough enough to take it. He yelled at everyone except Ryder, but no one got it as bad as I did.

I hated my life. I cried myself to sleep. I missed New Mexico.

Despite how "bad" I supposedly was at the game, I'd managed to help us reach the local midseason playoffs. This fact gave me no joy; I knew even if we won I'd get no reprieve, and we'd still have a month's worth of games ahead of us.

On the morning of the game in question, I didn't see how it would be possible for me to drag myself into my rank uniform. I'd refused to let Mom wash it, even though the material gave me rashes and it stank like the homeless people I used to see downtown, with caked-in sweat, dampened and dried, sticking to my skin like a graft.

It was the sort of day when, if you loved what you were doing, the bright sunshine and clear skies made it perfect, but if you dreaded what you were doing, the bright sunshine and clear skies made your experience even worse: sharper and clearer, impossible to deny.

Adding to my misery was the fact that, unbeknownst to me, Coach had ordered everyone to ask their mothers to wash their uniforms the night before this particular game. I showed up according to the previous rules, looking like a slob in front of all the other parents and saw them lean in to one another in a gossiping frenzy, wondering what things must be like at home.

My own parents weren't at the game because I'd told them it was a boring double-practice day.

Somehow, I made it to the top of the ninth without incident. My teammates' uniforms had acquired roughly the same amount of filth as mine, so at last I looked like a member of the group.

The visiting team was leading, 1–0. There were two outs, with no one on base. The batter hit a line drive to center field, which was where I was playing, and I held out my glove to catch the ball. But the ball hit the heel and landed on the grass near my feet. I picked it up and threw it back to the infield as quickly as I could, but not before the runner reached first.

The next batter hit a fly ball to Ryder, who was playing left field. He glided over toward the line and made the catch easily. He and the rest of the guys headed toward the dugout en masse, but I trudged slowly by myself, listening to Coach berate me the whole way.

"What was that?" he called out to me, shaking his head with disgust. "You couldn't catch a beach ball." That was unfair and I knew it. In New Mexico, I was a decent player. But you're only as good as your last game, and in all my games under Coach Tierson I couldn't do anything right, because I was shaking with fear.

He decided to use our final at-bat for an announcement, which he delivered in a hoarse voice. "All right, listen up. If anyone throws his bat from now on, you're off the team. Walk off the fucking field and don't come back. You're done. You won't finish the season, you won't play next year. I've had it. If you can't follow that one simple instruction I've got no use for you."

Everyone knew he was talking about me. I was a pariah. No one sat near me, Contagious Charlie, the freak.

I wasn't going to have a single friend come fall. I'd just moved here and I was already done.

Then Ryder got up to bat.

It was the bottom of the ninth and we were down a run.

The first pitch came in. Meatball. On a platter. Served up with a big "Hit me!" sign.

Easy home run—well, easy for someone like Ryder.

Yes, he knocked it out of the park.

Tied game, just like that.

All the guys leapt off the bench in a line of whoops, screaming, cheering, waving their caps. We could still win now. The day was saved.

But Ryder didn't move.

He just stood there and watched the ball fade into the distance.

"Go! Go!" people screamed. The crowd waved their arms frantically, stood up from their seats, called out to him. This was back when his parents were still together, so they were there. So was Griffin.

Ryder looked at the crowd, and then he looked at Coach, and

then he slowly wound up and threw his bat in a huge arc, so there was no mistaking it. It smacked against the chain-link fence right near the visiting team's dugout.

Despite devouring Dad's comic book collection, I'd never believed in superheroes before, not really, but now I knew. They were rare, but they existed.

Ryder slowly circled the bases, and when he got back to our dugout, he looked Coach dead in the eye, daring him to say something. But Coach's mouth was open; he was dumbfounded and speechless for once.

Ryder walked casually along the bench to where I sat, by myself. He stopped in front of me. "Are you coming?"

I smiled so hard, I thought my teeth would shatter and puncture my mouth, like clay plates shot into pieces in the air.

We chucked all our gear to the ground: helmets, gloves, protective padding; shed it all right there like we were already at home, and then we took off, walking, not running, *walking off the fucking field*, the way Coach had told us to. And we never looked back.

THE OTHER MARIA

ON THE WALK BACK TO SCHOOL, MY VISION WAVERED AND I swore I could see little pools of water on the black pavement up ahead, but every time I got close to them, they disappeared. I knew I would never reach them no matter how far or how long I walked.

I passed the Oasis Spa. There was no water in Palm Valley, yet all the businesses had names designed to make you think of life and springs and gardens, instead of rocks or tumbleweeds or dirt and sand and blisters.

Why didn't those damn European settlers go a little bit farther? I wondered, for what felt like the millionth time. If they'd toughed it out fifty or sixty miles south, maybe I'd be living in Santa Monica right now. Why did they stop here and dig their feet in? Did they convince themselves on a daily basis that the ocean really was just around the corner?

If a mirage makes you see things that aren't there, in Palm Valley you see things that *are really there but shouldn't be*. There shouldn't be a golf course, flowers, or any kind of tree, Joshua or otherwise. Everything shipped in from the outside, from LA or Colorado or wherever, didn't belong and never would have grown there naturally.

I shoved the school doors open and saw Ellie far down the hallway, looking like a tall drink of water at the end of a long, hot road. I was dying of thirst. I leaned over to drink a gallon from the fountain, but it didn't put a dent in my need; and when I looked up again, Ellie was gone, and I knew I had to stop. Drinking. If I really wanted to win her back, I had to cut that shit out.

I regretted my liquid lunch, wanted nothing more than to go back in time and have a Coke or a water at Ryder's instead. My brain was fuzzy and dry like a cactus, and it held things inside I couldn't access while I was tipsy. I just wanted to be clearheaded again. I wanted to be someone she could love.

I didn't know what to do about Griffin and his cap. Flynn Scientific was the military supplier where his father used to work. It matched the deputies' description of the person driving my car, but plenty of people wore a cap like that, and why on earth would Griffin have been at a high school choir party?

I made it through the end of the school day, and I even made it through practice without feeling too sick. I focused on my footwork, practiced headers, and kept to myself. I couldn't look a single one of my teammates in the eyes—not after I'd been approached to the throw the game. They had a potential traitor in their midst and they didn't even know it. The worst part was, I was actually considering it. What was one game, in the grand scheme of things? One game to help Ryder leave behind a miserable life? I told myself it wasn't about lining my pockets, but I didn't believe me.

As practice wore on, and I saw Patrick diving and throwing

himself into amazing deflections and saves, I changed my mind again. There was no way I could betray him like that. He was a great keeper who deserved a scholarship. My college future was all set—but he needed this, and it was my job to defend him. He should be able to count on me to try, at the very least.

I called my parents and left a message reminding them I'd be visiting Granddad, and then I took the bus over to the hospital in Lancaster. I was, apparently, all about the bus these days. The city bus was even worse than Palm Valley High's. It bounced and jangled and clanked over every pothole, shooting sparks of pain up my spine. The driver had long since stopped caring. Maybe his seat was more cushioned than the rest of ours, or at least his ass was.

I signed in at the visitors' station. Granddad was slowly getting over his pneumonia, so he was trapped in the sick ward of the hospital, but once he got better he'd be moving to a room at the active seniors' residence in the building next door.

He'd lived his whole life in nearby Quartz Hill, where he raised my dad.

Quartz Hill. Now, there was a town that knew when to fold. Back in the 1970s, Granddad inherited his parents' almond farm, just in time for the water source from LA to dry up completely. Everyone's crops died, Quartz Hill gave up, and all the farmers there decided to work for Lockheed Martin aerospace instead, Granddad included. The only acknowledgment of Quartz Hill's past was its annual Almond Blossom Festival. I'd taken Ellie to it last year.

At least Quartz Hill acted like a desert. Palm Valley still had blinders on.

Granddad's house was now up for sale, and most of his possessions were in our garage. My parents had offered to put him up at Chez Dixon while he fielded offers on his place, but like me, he liked his autonomy, or at least the illusion of it. And besides, there were no offers yet to field.

The "active seniors" Granddad would be cavorting with after his release from the hospital were 80 percent women, which I guess he liked, but I couldn't help thinking they were all widows, and how sad that was.

Conversation overheard in the waiting area of the hospital:

"My doctor says never to eat popcorn or peanuts because it's *murder* on the digestive system, just makes tiny cuts all the way down."

"That's appetizing. Of course, if you chew before swallowing—"

"My dog eats peanuts and he's all right."

"Yeah, well, dogs'll eat anything."

"Remember that dog that ate that *knife*? It was up on the table and it ate the whole birthday cake and then it ate the knife next to it that was used to cut the slices."

I was thinking of eating a knife right about then. No wonder Granddad drank, if that was the level of conversation he was subjected to.

He had other ways of coping besides drinking. Today he decided to share with me a box of vintage porn, which one of his buddies had brought over. The magazines had names like *Ace* and *Bachelor*.

"I tried the Internet the other day," Granddad admitted. "Before I got sick. Typed in 'nude beauties.' Not only could you see all there was to see, but it wasn't worth seeing. Harsh lighting, no mystery. No real curves, either." He smoothed out one of his magazines. "This is much sexier. I feel bad for you kids today. Twenty years ago you still had to *work* a little if you wanted to catch a peek; and the women were beautiful. Now you just turn on the computer and you can see people doing terrible things to each other right off the bat. There's nothing to it. Where's the mystery? Where's the anticipation? At least the lingerie catalogs still cover 'em up."

He had a point, I guess. But it's not like the Internet was a box you could close or a light you could turn off. It was always going to be there.

He smiled, adjusted his glasses. "I guess it sounds like I'm preaching. Laughing at your old fool of a grandpa?"

"No, it's just . . . Ellie would probably agree with you."

"Ellie's a smart girl. How'd she like the almond festival? I meant to ask."

"She gave it an 8.5."

"She *rated* your date?"

"Yep."

"You ever get a 10?"

I smiled and shook my head. "Gotta have something to aim for, right?"

Granddad gave me a long look. "If you say so."

He pulled a bottle of Jameson out from the box. The magazines had been used to smuggle it in. "Need a fill-up?"

"I'm okay today—I gotta keep my head about me," I said.

"What's on your mind?"

I slouched in my seat. "I don't even know where to start." The party? Ryder and the history window? The soccer match? The girl? Always, the girl?

"School got you down? Tough to be back after that long vacation?" he asked gently.

"I guess I feel like I'm running out of time. I graduate in a few months, and then I have to decide how I want to spend the rest of my life. How am I supposed to know? The only thing I was ever sure about was Ellie—and I thought—I really thought the rest of it would fall into place if she was with me. But she doesn't feel the same way." Suddenly I did want a fill-up.

"Why should you know what you're going to do at age eighteen? Why should you know how you want to spend the next fifty years of your life when you haven't known anything but schooling? And why should you know who you want to be with?"

"But I *do* know. That's the problem."

It was nice telling him all that, even if he didn't have a solution. It was his lack of solutions that proved he'd been listening.

Mom and Dad would've gotten out the Lambert College course catalog and made me walk through it like it was all an exciting quest: The Mystery of Charlie's Future. Like I'd literally meant I needed help deciding how to spend my life, so now we were sitting down as a family and figuring it out before dinner; they'd have had at me until I'd given them a false smile.

They wanted so badly for me to be okay, so they could be okay. The pressure of it was enough to crack concrete.

I hung around for another hour, learning gin rummy and watching Granddad's hands, gnarled but steady, deal the cards. He always gave the cards a little topspin and flip as he tossed them in my direction. He looked pretty wiped out, though, and my homework wasn't going to write itself, so with reluctance I said good-bye, picked up my backpack (now containing an issue of *Ace*), and headed out to the hallway.

When I passed by the last room on the right, I heard someone crying and moaning. I crept closer and peeked through the door to make sure a nurse or doctor was tending to the patient.

The patient was Maria Salvador, in the throes of hallucination, rocking back and forth at the edge of her bed, holding a nurse's hand.

Her head wobbled around like it was off its hinges. She was wild-eyed, swiveling; part of her face looked like it wanted to get away from the other part.

I remembered her sad, hollow eyes from the party on Sunday. She was a pretty Hispanic girl with thick hair, small, chapped lips, and gorgeous eyelashes. In the hospital light, I vaguely recognized her from the caf, from songbird events, from a solo last year. She didn't belong here, tripping her brains out.

"The walls," she moaned, slapping her hand against the wall

closest to her bed. She was looking at me but seeing God only knows what. "They're breathing. They always breathed, didn't they? I just never noticed before."

"She hasn't had too many visitors, just her family," said the nurse holding her hand. "Do you go to school with her?"

"Yeah. Thought I'd stop in."

The poor girl was clutching something in her hand and murmuring to herself. "The kiss," she said. "In exile. In exile."

I was stuck in quicksand, rooted to the spot, like all the people who hadn't meant to but found themselves in Palm Valley, California. I couldn't lift my feet again to keep heading west. I don't care what people say; it's as hard to leave misery as it is to leave happiness.

Why had no one from school visited her yet?

"What's in her hand?" I said in order to say something. Anything.

"A key chain. She won't let go of it," the nurse said. "I think it comforts her, but it's leaving a mark in her palm."

"Sugar. Bup bup bup bup bup bup. Oh, honey, honey. You are my candy girl," Maria sang, woeful and warbled.

"Is she ever going to stop hallucinating?" I asked. How much had she taken?

"We're keeping her hydrated and safe, and hoping for the best for now," said the nurse, though I wasn't sure what the nurse meant by "her."

Because there was no "her" left. Whoever Maria Salvador used to be, she was gone.

THE COUNTEROFFER

WHEN I GOT HOME, ALL THE WINDOWS IN ALL THE HOUSES on my block had their lights on. Every rectangle and square glowed, both floors, top to bottom. It was the opposite of the school at night, and combated some of my gloom. I stared, mesmerized and comforted, until I realized the uniform golden blaze lighting up every window was nothing more than a reflection from the fading sun, about to disappear.

I did my homework for a couple hours, then changed for bed and emptied my pockets.

Out came the folded note written on Ellie's stationery.

Out came the message I'd ripped from the school newspaper. "To ChD. If you find it, don't give it to her. I'll pay more. IM 10 2nite."

It was 9:45. I turned on my computer and logged on to my IM account.

I knew what I had to do.

Whoever this guy was, he assumed Bridget was paying me to find the drive, or he wouldn't have offered to beat the price. I could shake him down for anything, since he didn't know money had never been part of the equation. I could walk away from Bridget *and* Ryder, win Ellie back for doing so, and just report to this mystery guy from now on for one big payoff.

At 9:59, my computer beeped. *BM has sent you a message. Do you accept?*

I clicked Yes and when the chat window opened, I cut to the chase:

Charlie: Who is this?

BM: Do you have the flash drive?

Charlie: Not yet, but I'm close.

BM: How close?

Charlie: Who is this?

BM: Not so fast.

Charlie: You'll have to tell me eventually.

No reply. Thirty, forty, fifty seconds went by.

Charlie: How much money are we talking about?

BM: Double whatever she's paying.

It was my turn to pause. Ryder had offered to pay me five hundred bucks for fouling Steve at the soccer game and giving him a penalty kick. Why not start there? Before I could type $250 so BM would double it to $500, BM panicked, apparently believing I was stalling as some kind of negotiating tactic. I hate to brag, but I'm not that smart.

BM: I'll give you as much as I can.

Charlie: $1,000

BM: She's paying you $1,000? That's all?

(Dammit, dammit, I'd lowballed.)

Charlie: Yeah, so double is $2,000.

BM: I can multiply.

Charlie: Don't get snippy.

BM: How close are you really?

Charlie: I'm getting there. Eliminating suspects.

BM: You know about the lady with the dog?

Charlie: Who's that?

BM: I thought you worked at the library.

Charlie: I do.

BM: Look, no more games. I'm good for the money. Just don't give it to her, okay? You can't give it to her.

Charlie: No worries. I'm done dealing with Bridget.

BM: ??

I stared at the screen. It felt like we were having two different conversations.

Charlie: What do you mean "??"

Long pause.

BM: I wasn't talking about Bridget.

Charlie: Then who?

BM has signed off.

I cursed myself for denying Granddad's flask fill-up. If that IM conversation had been any more confusing, I might as well have been drunk for it.

Mostly I was sick of going alone on this. It'd only been two days and I was already having trouble keeping track of the players.

I wrote a quick chart.

Bridget — Wants her flash drive back, which may not be hers; claims it was stolen out of the library 2nd period last Friday, when she may not have been there. Claims it has a college scholarship essay on it. Is probably lying about A) everything

BM — Wants flash drive, and is willing to pay $2,000 for it, which he thinks is a steal (!). Is under the impression I've been dealing with a girl other than Bridget.

Ryder — Wants me to forget about the flash drive.*

Maria Posey — Was at the library last Friday getting tutoring. Has a thing with Ryder? Wanted him to do a favor for her, but he said no. Hates the Other Maria for "stealing" her solos.

Other Maria — overdosed on LSD; has been hallucinating since Sunday night; no one seems to care

Danny — Bridget's li'l stalker who may come in handy

Ellie / Ellie Plagiarist — Wants me to think Ellie is blackmailing Bridget

Car thief (Griffin?) — Wanted the cops to think I dosed Maria Salvador

*Best option so far

Everyone needed someone else to bounce ideas off of. Sherlock had Watson. Kirk had Spock. In *Fast & the Furious*, Brian O'Conner had Dominic Toretto. And like Granddad said, Ellie was smart.

I picked up the phone and dialed. Ellie answered on the third ring. The clock read 10:18.

"Two nights in a row?" was her greeting.

"Too late to call?"

"Never was before."

She told me once she loved hearing my voice as the very last one before she fell asleep. She said her day wasn't complete unless she'd told me about it.

Sometimes we'd kept our phones on even when we weren't talking, even when we were trying to drift off. (*"You still there?"* / *"Yeah, you?"* / *"Yeah."*) Not the wittiest banter in the world, but it was ours.

"Wasn't sure if the rules had changed," I said. "But here we are."

"You can't keep calling me," she said.

"You're the one who called me yesterday," I pointed out.

"To explain why you couldn't keep calling me."

"And our date tomorrow? Is that to further explain?"

"It's not a date. Think of it as a way for Jonathan to say good-bye."

"And yet you haven't hung up."

"I—"

"Any idea why someone would want to frame you?" I said.

"Frame me? For what?"

I read her the note.

"I didn't write that," she said, sounding perplexed. "And I don't know what it means."

"Yeah. It's a pretty good forgery, and it's on your stationery, but you never call me 'Dix.' " I'd spent part of the day mulling things over in my head, and wondering what Ellie was hiding from me, but in the end it didn't make sense. Only Bridget called me that. Either *she'd* forged the note (but why?) or the person who had was close to Bridget and believed both my exes used the same nickname for me. Maybe I should thank the person; it'd given me a reason to call Ellie.

"Where'd you get it?" Ellie said.

"Doesn't matter, anymore," I said, crumpling the paper up.

"There was a sale at Pens 'n' More at the mall last week. Anyone could've bought that stationery."

"Okay. Good to know."

"Now that you've cleared my name, is that all?"

"I don't know. Are you done running hot and cold?"

"Are you done taking a bath in it?" she said.

"I saw Maria Salvador today," I remarked, without missing a beat.

"I didn't know you two were friends," said Ellie. "Is she doing better?"

"I was visiting my granddad, and she was down the hall at the hospital. The nurse said no one's visited her besides family."

"I wasn't sure they were letting anyone see her. Shit. Now I wish I'd gone, too."

"She's in pretty bad shape, muttering to herself, not making any sense, saying weird phrases like 'In exile.' She kept repeating that. And singing that song 'Sugar, Sugar.' It was really messed up."

"That was in our medley of sixties harmonies for the qualifier in Pomona over New Year's. Maybe it got stuck in her head?" Ellie wondered. "God. I feel so bad for her. Do they have any idea who dosed her yet?"

"Not that I know of. Any idea who the lady with the dog is?"

"You should signal when you make a weird turn like that."

"My conversational segues have gotten rusty without our nightly calls," I said. "You have no one to blame but yourself."

"It's not a who, it's a what. The title of a Chekhov story."

"What's it about?"

"A young woman with a Pomeranian and this old dude she has an affair with. I probably misinterpreted it. I hope so, anyway."

"Why's that?"

"Just once I want to read about an old woman and a young man."

"But that would be gross," I teased.

"Uh-huh," she said drily. "Why so curious about the chekhovs?"

"I'm following a tip. Do they meet in the library or something?" BM had acted like I should know about them simply because I was doing time there.

"There's a section in the library that's only available to students in the AP Chekhov class."

"It's restricted? Off-limits?"

She laughed. "It's not dark magic, it's just that the books are falling apart. They're from the seventies. You have to prove you're in the class before you can look at them. Not that anyone else would want to."

"Got it," I said, though I didn't. "Can I say one more thing?"

"Sure."

She was in a better mood now, so I took a risk and came clean. "Ryder's been stealing test answers and selling them. That's why he needed the window unlocked. I didn't know before, but now that I do, I'm not helping him anymore. I just wanted you to know."

Silence.

"Well . . . now I know."

"So we're cool with the Ryder thing?"

"I mean, I'm not *thrilled*, but yeah, we're cool with the Ryder thing."

One issue down, two to go: soccer and college. "And we're still on for tomorrow night?"

"Seven. Jonathan and I expect you to wear a film-related costume. And it can't be half-assed. Start sewing."

Click.

I smiled at the dial tone and set the phone down. In my dreams I continued to hear her voice, all soft and teasing, like strings of possibility dangling from the ceiling. All I had to do was pull, and a trap door would open, and I could walk up the ladder and back into her arms.

THE OBVIOUS HIDING PLACE

ON WEDNESDAY MORNING, I TOOK THE BUS AGAIN AND IT was the same old thing, most of it involving the petty destruction of property. Freshman boys in hoodies drew on their seat backs with pen, digging in deep; freshman girls in hoodies made ironic friendship bracelets by piercing their seats with safety pins and tying embroidery floss in intricate patterns.

The driver bleated at us. The radio broadcast static. The potholes got revenge for decades of tyranny. The bus cut off commuters. It had been doing this for twenty years and would continue doing it for another twenty.

You never forgot you were on a bus. iPhones and headphones could block out a lot of things, but the bus was not one of them. You were always aware of the smell of green plastic and burned rubber, and the squeaky door handle rusting on its hinge as it slowly opened and closed to accept more mass onto the rolling amoeba.

The bus never took you where you really wanted to go. The bus never took you anywhere at all. What it did was take you in circles, from home to school and school to home. At least in your car, there was a chance you could escape the loop, veer off the track, head to Vegas. You'd never do it, but there was a chance.

For the first time since my sentence was handed out, I full-on hustled to the library. My hustling was all the more interesting considering I wasn't scheduled to be there. I had to work fast before Mr. Minnow, the long-faced part-time librarian, arrived.

I was supposed to have familiarized myself with the library layout by now, as part of my punishment, so I could be a better font of information, but I still needed the crib sheet. I pulled out the laminated map and studied it. History. Literature. Science. Math. English. Spanish. And then, in tiny, smudged letters in the corner, nearest to Bridget's supposed location at the time of the theft, the Chekhov section.

The "section" was nothing more than a small glass case in the back of the library, completely unobtrusive, not even remotely tempting. I figured it'd at least have a sign up saying "Do Not Touch! Part of living museum!" or something. There were about ten books, some duplicates, including plays and short-story anthologies by Chekhov, all under lock and key, like the high-end liquor aisle at Vons.

I darted back to the info desk and fumbled through the drawers, looking for the key. Mr. Minnow walked in and asked what I was doing. Librarians were among the first casualties of the budget wars, so he only came in three times a week. I think he subsidized his lack of pay by stealing truckloads of coffee and croissants from the teachers' lounge; he always had two huge thermoses with him.

"Extra-credit project. I'm researching Chekhov," I replied.

He squinted at me, scanning me like a bar code. "Okay, I'll go with you."

The last thing I needed was him standing over my shoulder, but I didn't have a choice. He had a strung-together key chain in his pocket. He flicked through it and located the right one, then opened the cabinet.

I knelt down and quickly read the titles. I didn't remember if "The Lady with the Dog" was a play, a novel, or a short story, so I grabbed a collection of selected shorts first, and opened to the table of contents.

The Confession

Surgery

A Cure for Drinking (might be useful)

In Spring

Three Years

In Exile

The Darling

The Kiss

"In Exile"? "The Kiss"? Maria Salvador hadn't been speaking gibberish, or talking about herself when I'd seen her in the hospital. She'd been listing Chekhov titles. What was the connection?

"Gently, gently," Mr. Minnow drawled, as I hurried through the next collection. And there it was . . .

"The Lady with the Dog." I flipped through the pages, looking for highlighted words, underlined passages, anything to tell me why it was a clue. Nothing. I turned the book over, checked the front and back flaps, even the stamped pocket where library tickets used to go in the 1970s.

"*What* are you doing?" demanded Mr. Minnow.

I rotated the book in my hands, feeling it up like we were alone in the back of a car. The binding on the book was loose; the spine had shifted away from the pages, exposing a gap.

The gap was the exact shape and size of a flash drive.

But if the flash drive had been hidden there, it was gone now, just like Maria Salvador's mind. Someone had beaten me to it.

Jane Thomas (a.k.a. Thomas' English Muffin) sat at her computer in the journalism room, clicking through images for next week's issue of the *Palm Valley High Recorder*. She was our cute British transplant who'd taken over the school newspaper and turned it into a must-read tabloid. She was Rupert Murdoch in a jean skirt and loafers, presumably minus the phone hacking. Our paper may have been respectable before, but it sure was boring. And actually it had never been respectable.

She jumped when I strolled in; the bell hadn't rung yet and she clearly wasn't expecting visitors. In fact, her hand clicked and shifted the mouse in such a way that if those sites weren't blocked, I might've thought she was closing out of a porn site.

I pretended I hadn't seen, and I reminded her who I was. I was on a mission, but I couldn't ignore protocol. As fellow seniors, we could interact as long as there had been a previous introduction.

"Hi, Jane, we met through my dad, he writes a column for the *Press* and teaches over at Lambert College?"

She looked up. "Right. You're a footballer. What's on your mind?"

"We prefer beckhams."

"And *we* prefer if you leave that sport to those who know how to play it. FYI, Becks is retired."

"Beckham's the only soccer player everyone knows."

"Pelé was voted footballer of the century. Why not call yourself the pelés?"

I shrugged. "I just play the game, I don't follow it."

"You Americans think soccer is nothing but a sport for children."

"You and I both know it's the opposite," I teased.

"Cheeky."

"You don't really say words like 'cheeky.'"

"Guv'nor," she said.

"You're totally mocking. You just think that's what I think you talk like."

"And why would I bother putting on a show?"

"To distract me from the reason I'm here. Someone left a message in your paper yesterday and I can't figure out who it's from," I said.

She gave me a lengthy once-over. "Lovelorn girl?"

"Not exactly. Well—maybe." It was a good point. Maybe BM wasn't a he. And playing the part of a thwarted lover might endear me to Jane. "Can you help me out?"

"What was the message?"

"'To ChD, if you find it, don't give it to her. I'll pay more. IM 10 2nite.'"

Jane rolled her eyes. "Hmm, yes. Bartering for goods and services is extremely romantic."

"So I jump online at the designated time and—"

"Pull a Craigslist Killer. We all do it."

"I'm ... pretty sure we don't," I said.

"It's just an expression."

"I'm pretty sure it's not."

She grinned. "Lifetime movie. Means you used false pretenses to get information from someone."

"Can you help me out? Tell me who sent the message?"

"Absolutely not. Journalistic ethics."

"I have a secret for you. I'd hardly call this place a hotbed of journalism," I stage-whispered behind my hand. "And I'd hardly call the gossip pages solid reporting."

"It gets the paper read," she said matter-of-factly. "I don't mind if people pick it up for the gossip; it means they might also read my exposé on the cafeteria contracts. Besides, if people know their identities will be leaked, they won't use the service. I can't tell you who placed the call."

I straightened up. "You deserve better than this. Why not work for the *Palm Valley Register*? I'm sure my dad could put in a good word," I said. "*If* you help out his one and only darling son, Charlie." I clasped my hands together and did my best impersonation of a puppy dog with a bow around its neck.

"You being the darling in question?"

"I love your accent. It's like you're insulting me, but I barely notice."

She folded her arms. "And what does my posture tell you?"

I sighed. "A sentry at the gate."

I acted like I was about to leave, and she turned back to her computer. Then I slipped behind her desk and looked over her shoulder at the screen.

"What are you doing?" she cried, trying to cover the monitor with her hands. She managed to X out of the site, but not before I'd seen a list of ID numbers scrolling by.

"You're Bridget's source, aren't you?" I said.

"I have literally no idea what you're talking about."

"You're the one who matches the ID numbers to the student names. Did you hack into the registration office, or did you get someone else to do your dirty work?"

Her face went red, but she stuck to her denials. "It's not what you think."

"So much for journalistic ethics," I scoffed.

"I'm compiling a story for the paper about college. How many people applied to which schools, what percent are Ivy League, what percent are local, that sort of thing. I got *permission* from Principal Jeffries to use the information, so long as I keep all the names out. It's part of their initiative to prove the impact of Fresh Start, and, by the way, it directly impacts your mother's job security. No student names will be revealed."

"How can you tell where people applied?" I asked.

"It's all there in their student profile. Electronic receipts showing where transcripts, recommendation letters, and applications have been e-mailed."

I felt ill.

Five minutes alone with that list and I could find out where Ellie had applied, once and for all. Had she sent materials to Lambert, or was she lying about that? Had she ever loved me, or was this her exit strategy from day one: string Charlie along, pretend you might stay together after high school, but always remember he's not good enough to plan a real future with. If she *had* applied, there was still a good chance for us. If not . . . maybe I didn't want to know.

"You're good," I said. "You and Bridget should go into business."

Jane looked insulted. "I'm not *profiting* from it. It's for an article."

"Everything's for sale," I told her. "What's the going rate to look at another student's transcript file?"

"I'm going to forget you asked me that," she said, and shut down her computer.

During third period, I was scheduled to meet with Palm Valley High's guidance counselor to follow up on my plans for college. It was a pointless exercise and I treated it as such.

Ms. Gerard had pushed her desk to the wall and set up a cozy "we're all friends here" couch and chair, with a snack-covered coffee table between us. I sat down across from her.

"Lambert's my first choice, my backup, and my safety. Cool, huh? See you at graduation."

I stood up.

"Sounds like you think everything's set in stone," Ms. Gerard said. She was a serious-looking blonde in an argyle sweater vest and glasses, just one makeover and hair toss away from being voted Hottest Faculty Member. The sweater vest and glasses were a feeble attempt at staving off that title. "How do you feel about that?"

I reluctantly sat again, stretching out on the couch. "Are you a guidance counselor or a failed psychiatrist?" I said.

She looked at me for a second, and then laughed. Barely. It was one of those laughs that tells you to back off. "You don't seem very enthusiastic. Is there someplace else you'd like to go? Plenty of places have rolling admissions policies."

"It just makes sense. Why spend a fortune when I can get a perfectly good education almost for free?"

"Just because something makes sense isn't reason enough to do it."

"Does Lambert know you're actively discouraging students from attending? Should I alert the chancellor?"

She set her pencil down. I pictured it sticking upright in the table like a thrown knife. "Okay, Charlie. Are you going to take this seriously or shall I call in the next student?"

"Look, I appreciate what you're doing, but it's settled. I was going to live at my granddad's, get some space from my parents, but now he's selling the place. So yeah, I'm bummed about that, but the thing is, I don't have any money. My parents are footing the bill, so they should have a say, don't you think?"

"Could they foot the bill someplace else?"

"For ten times the price?" I said sarcastically. "Right now they've set aside forty grand in a money market account for me. With my dad's discount, and no room or board, that's four years at Lambert including classes, supplies, and textbooks. Or I could spend a *month* at some other school."

"What about scholarships?"

"You really don't want me to go to Lambert," I remarked. "You're obsessed."

"It's not about what I want. It's about what you want. If you could go anywhere on the planet, forget about cost or logistics or what 'makes sense,' where would you go?"

"Wherever Ellie is," I said without thinking.

If Ms. Gerard *were* a failed psychiatrist, it was only because she'd dropped out a week before graduation to follow Phish on tour or something. I'd walked right into her trap. Sneaky.

"Who's Ellie?"

"Ellie Chen. Drop-dead gorgeous Chinese girl. Did you meet with her yet?"

"We met on Tuesday," Ms. Gerard said guardedly.

"Can you tell me—"

"No."

"You don't even know what I'm going to ask yet."

"I can't tell you where she's going."

"But you know, don't you?"

"I want to help you, Charlie, but you're making things really difficult. If you only take one thing from this session today—"

"Ennui and disaffection?"

"Let it be that you have a say in your own life. If you truly want to go to Lambert, go. But if you don't, I'd be happy to call your parents and we can all sit down together and discuss other possibilities."

All four of us could sit down, but only three of us would talk. I wasn't sure I wanted to add Ms. Gerard to the cast of "Analyze Charlie," now on tour for a special matinee performance, one day only.

Patrick, goalkeeper and head beckham, was waiting for me at my locker after lunch.

"How's it going?" I asked.

We bumped fists.

"Fine," said Patrick. "Feeling okay for practice today?"

"Yeah, I'm good. What's up?"

"Got a second to speak to some cherkoff? He didn't say what it's about, just said you'd want to know. What the eff, right? If you don't care, I'll tell him to get lost."

"No, it's cool. I can talk to him. Thanks."

Patrick walked around the corner and returned with a plump African American kid. "Phil, Charlie. Charlie, Phil," he intro'd. "Bell's in thirty, buckaroos. Keep it clean."

I nodded at Patrick to take off. The African American kid offered his hand. "I'm Phil."

"I gathered that."

"I saw you at no-man's-land looking through our books."

"And?"

"Was it yours? Did you put the flash drive there?"

"BM?" I asked.

"Huh?"

"Never mind."

"Because I found a flash drive there on Monday. I was copying down a passage for my paper, and the flash drive fell out. When I saw you looking, I figured it was yours, and you were hiding it there for safekeeping."

"What'd you do with it?" I asked, heart pounding. "When it fell out, what'd you do with it?"

He looked at me as though it were obvious. "I—I put it in lost and found. Gave it to the old bat in Jeffries's office."

I was dumbfounded. "You put it in lost and found."

"Yeah, you can go pick it up anytime. So . . . no harm, no foul?"

Damn Phil and his normalcy! Didn't he know half the school was interested in the flipping thing? Of course, before Monday, I would've done the same thing. Bridget had me so convinced people were liars and thieves—well, some of them were, namely Bridget—that it had never occurred to me to look in lost and found. Two days wasted when all I had to do was act legit and stroll into the principal's office and ask for the flash drive!

I grasped Phil's shoulder, spoke swiftly and quietly. "Does anyone else know? Think carefully."

At my behest, the "old bat" (a.k.a. Mrs. Batiglio) behind the counter ambled over to Principal Jeffries's office and returned with the lost and found bin. Inside were a jacket, a couple of notebooks, a Trapper Keeper, an iPhone or two, even some nice-looking pens. I thought she'd set the plastic bin on the table and I could sift through it and grab the flash drive, but instead, she kept it out of arm's length from me, reached inside, cupped something in her palm, peeked at it, and reburied it.

"You're in luck," she said. "We have a flash drive."

"Oh, thank the Lord. That's such a relief," I feigned, pleased with my acting. I could've joined drama freshman year, if I'd lacked sufficient parental-and-peer attention, of course, the prerequisite for stage monkeys.

"There's a sticker on it," the Old Bat informed me. "Tell me what the sticker is and you can have it back."

Freaking seriously? What *sticker* was on it? "Uh . . ." I squinted. "I'm not sure I remember."

"Well, when you do remember, you can have it back."

"What if I tell you what's *in* the flash drive and you look it up on your computer and see that I'm right?"

"I can't do that."

"How come?"

"That would be a violation of your privacy."

"I don't mind." I gave her my biggest, cheesiest grin.

"The sticker."

"Let me get back to you. I'll just . . . go through all my other stickered flash drives and use the process of elimination," I grumbled.

Too Fast, Too Furious, I wheeled around and plowed through the doors into the hall. Danny was actually waiting for me by the water fountain, just as I'd asked the other day. Underclassmen had their uses.

"Okay, here's what's going down," I said. "Do you need to take notes, or can you memorize this?"

Danny dutifully flipped open his sketch pad and poised his charcoal.

"I need you to get a message to the drama kids. I need you to tell them I'll be doing a perp walk *tomorrow* between second and third, right down this hall, should they want revenge."

Danny hadn't written a word. He cocked his head curiously at me. "Revenge for what?"

"It'll be obvious. After it goes down, that's what you tell them. 'Charlie Dixon is doing a perp walk between second and third tomorrow.' Got it?"

Just before seventh I cornered Bridget outside European history, for what I hoped would be our last meeting. I knew that's where she'd be because I'd memorized a few spots on her schedule last time we'd talked.

"What sticker's on the flash drive?" I demanded.

"Jeez, you scared me." She placed her hand where she probably assumed her heart was, like a Southern belle with the vapors. "You're getting stalkery, Charlie. And not in a hot way."

"The sticker?"

"What're you babbling about?" she said.

I made a noise of frustration. "You don't even know what's on the flash drive, do you? You definitely don't know what it looks like. So how'd you get messed up in this? What are you even doing?"

"Did you find it?" she asked, emerald eyes agleam, begging to be appraised.

"You're not listening to me."

"I listened, I just don't care. There's a difference."

I placed my arms on either side of her shoulders and leaned in. "What's on it?"

She pursed her lips and looked side to side, seeming to contemplate ducking under my arms or knocking them away. In the end she did neither.

"Look, I know where it is," I told her. "I just need to know what's *on* it. Literally, as in, what sticker, and also what file it really contains; but we both know you're never going to be straight with me about that."

She closed her eyes, heaved a sigh, and opened them again. "Fine. I was embarrassed. It's naked pictures of me."

I hooted. "You're lying."

"What makes you say that?"

"Your mouth's moving. Also, the way your mind works, you would have told me that in the first place, thinking I'd be so desperate to see the photos I'd have the flash drive back for you in a second." I got in her face. "Has anything you've told me about any of this been true?"

She didn't answer.

I backed off. "Doesn't matter. I'll have the flash drive this time tomorrow."

"Seriously?"

My plan was still forming, but I had twenty-four hours to perfect it. The important thing was getting Bridget to tell whoever she was working with that I had it, so I could draw him out of hiding. I didn't believe she was flying solo.

"Where should we meet?" Bridget wondered.

I feigned surprise. "Oh, it's not for you, Bridge. Not anymore. I'm gonna make *a lot* of money off this. But thanks for gettin' me on the case." I slapped her on the back, all friendly-like.

Her bottom lip dropped and her eyes flashed in anger. "But . . . I helped you. I got you out of trouble with the sheriff's department."

I placed my middle finger on her lips, which in retrospect was only flipping *myself* off. "Shh."

She swatted my finger away and I laughed.

It felt good to have the upper hand for once.

PHASE ONE

PHASE ONE OF MY PLAN TO BREAK INTO PRINCIPAL JEFFRIES'S office and steal the flash drive required that I declare war on the drama kids. Being drama kids, they were by definition easily hurt and vengeful, but I couldn't risk using a light touch. I needed to stage a scene so over the top they would secretly envy not writing, scoring, directing, lighting, or starring in it.

I'd be ten minutes late to soccer practice, so I pulled Josh aside after history and told him to let Coach and Patrick know I was on my way.

"I'll cover for you," said Josh, barely looking at me as he stacked his books in a pile. "For the game, too, if you want."

"What's that supposed to mean?"

"If you're not up for it."

"What's *that* supposed to mean?" I repeated.

Josh quickly shook his head. "Never mind. Patrick and I were talking about the Agua Dulce game. And we think maybe it's better if you sit this one out."

"Just today Patrick asked if I was fit for practice, and when I told him I was, he was cool with it. So that doesn't fly."

"Right, but . . ." He stopped packing up and rubbed his eyes before looking at me. "If you give me all ninety minutes this Friday, you can start any game you want for the rest of the season."

"I can do that anyway."

"Or you can bench me for good, whatever."

I pushed him in the shoulder. "That's not up to me!"

"You keep showing up late or drunk, what do you think's going to happen?" Josh said, shoving me back. "No one can rely on you. There's gonna be *scouts* at this game."

"I just need ten minutes today, all right? I'll be there, asshole," I muttered, and took off for the auditorium. I'm self-aware enough to know I was angry because everything he'd said was true, for more reasons than he knew. Even though I hadn't agreed to throw the game, the conversation I'd had with Ryder still haunted me.

The day's cafeteria theme food had been Mexicali. I'm proud to say the once-a-week "ethnic-educational" menu was *not* one of my mom's initiatives. I'd loaded up on tomatillos (little green tomatoes) and hid them in a plastic bag, which had probably stunk up my locker. Weapons collected, I crept up to the auditorium balcony to watch a dress rehearsal for the spring production of *The Misanthrope*.

The idea was to anger the drama kids, not hurt any of them. I'm not a deer hunter. I decided to prey on their most basic, cherished fears.

"This play sucks! No one likes it. Not even the junior high bloggers will review this lame excuse for a Molière," I yelled, and chucked tomatillos at the stage, over, under, and past the ducking, traumatized performers in French aristocrat costumes. I barely got five off when the harsh beam of a spotlight, wielded by a techie in the control booth, nailed me in the face. I took off down the back stairs, two at a time, and out onto the soccer field.

They'd stew in it—but they couldn't follow. They couldn't move fast enough to catch me, nor risk ruining their costumes, and even if they did catch up to me, they certainly weren't going to take on a team of jocks in broad daylight.

I was proud of my attack. Coach Tierson was dead wrong about me back in Little League. I had a *great* throwing arm, and perfect aim. The stage had been packed, but I hadn't hit a single kid; hadn't splattered a single costume.

JUST LIKE OLD TIMES

AFTER PRACTICE, I GRABBED A RIDE HOME WITH PATRICK.

"Josh wants me out of the game on Friday," I told him.

"Josh always wants you out of the game. Don't worry about it."

"What do you think?"

"I think you got dumped and took it hard. You're not the first, and you won't be the last. If you tell me you're good for Friday, I'll believe you."

"I'm good for Friday," I said.

He pulled up to my house. "What're you doing right now? Want to practice more?"

"Actually, I'm seeing a movie with my ex," I said sheepishly.

When Ellie rang the doorbell, I made sure I had plenty of gifts on hand. The pomegranates from Christmas had gone bad, so I'd grabbed a few fresh ones from Granddad's yard. I'd also bought a mini-cactus in a pot and a couple packets of Nerds for Jonathan, so he wouldn't need me to spend twelve dollars or whatever on popcorn. The tickets had set me back almost forty dollars as it was.

Ellie stared at the mini-cactus, confused. "Cute," she said, not taking it from me. "What is it? A metaphor?"

I set it down. "You never have to water it, and there's no commitment; it just lives in hope, in the worst possible conditions." I waited for her to catch my gaze. "Kinda like me."

"Ha. You didn't have to do that," she said.

She was wearing a tight camisole and a thin cardigan over an old pair of jeans. I knew the jeans intimately. I knew what it felt like to unzip them, tug them down her legs. I knew how soft and faded the denim was. I knew how warm and smooth her thighs were.

How many times had I kissed her, standing right in this spot? Hundreds? Thousands? Deep, soft, lingering kisses good night, neither of us wanting to be the first to break them off, both of us dragging the other person back under.

Maybe I should've kept one last nip of something handy, just to make it through the desert of Ellie.

Jonathan tore into the foyer and clapped his hands imperiously at us. "Chop-chop, or we'll be late."

He saw the cactus and did an about-face. "Hello, what's this?"

"When you have a date with a girl, you should never show up empty-handed," I said. "Even if she comes to your place."

"Oh God, is this the night you teach Jonathan how to impress the ladies?" Ellie teased.

"If this is our last date, it's my last chance to show him what to do."

"In that case, I graciously accept." She curtsied. "Thank you for the hideous cactus."

"Hideous? It's a desert flower."

"He got you this?" said Jonathan, reaching out to touch it. "Cool."

Ellie tried to stop him. "Don't, you'll—"

"Ow. Frogger!" He shook his hand out and sucked on his finger.

"You'll find that boys can't resist what they're not supposed to have," I remarked to Ellie as an aside, like I was live-narrating a documentary about a strange and wondrous species.

"Please, tell me more about these 'boys.' Like why they have to make everything so difficult."

I shrugged. "They just want to keep life interesting." I remembered Ms. Gerard, the guidance counselor, saying the same thing about me, that I made things difficult. Did all women use the same quote book?

"Tick-tock," said Jonathan, looking pointedly at his phone, braces catching the light. He was practically bouncing on the balls of his feet. He'd been waiting to see this film since the previous one came out, a year ago. One night when Ellie and I had nothing else planned (she'd dismissed my suggestions of mini-golf and bumper cars—admittedly conventional—as "Organized fun? Really, Charlie?"), he made us watch it on DVD. The acting was wooden, but the premise was pretty good. I'd promised to take him to the sequel, never in a million years thinking Ellie and I would be kaput by then. This should've been a regular evening, a given, one in a series of regular evenings, blurring together to form a relationship; instead, tonight stood outside of our relationship, looking in, face pressed up against the glass with longing.

"Should I try to make it all the way there without braking?" I asked Jonathan.

"Yeah!" Jonathan yelled from the backseat.

Last year it was a thing everyone was doing—going nowhere slowly. The rules were simple: You're never allowed to come to a complete stop, so if you see a yellow or red light ahead, you have to glide toward it infinitesimally, enraging everyone behind you. That's the real test, sustaining your resolve in the face of fury. Sometimes you're going an inch a minute, but as long as you're still moving, you're in the game. Before I got good at it, I'd end up almost a third of the way through an intersection before it mercifully turned green, Ellie laughing and slapping at my arm the whole time. The cops couldn't understand why every high schooler was suddenly rolling stop signs.

"Great," said Ellie, beside me. "Tell me again why I relinquished the right to drive my own car?"

"J-Dawg, this might be the most important lesson of dating. The guy should always drive."

"Oh, shut up," Ellie said.

"Why?" asked Jonathan.

"He thinks women are bad drivers," Ellie explained, and snorted.

"That's horrible. I would never think that. I think *Asians* are bad drivers," I said, and she swatted the back of my head. "Ow."

"So if I'm dating a white girl, does she drive or do I drive?" said Jonathan, perplexed.

"Go with your gut instinct," said Ellie. "If she says, 'Should I try to make it all the way there without braking?' *you* should drive."

"I've mastered no braking," I assured them both. "I'm better at it now."

And I was. It was beautiful. We coasted all the way to Palm Valley Mall without slowing; every traffic light rooted me on and smiled down at me. I gauged exactly when the lights were about to turn green, timed it to perfection, and coasted through each intersection at the right moment, sliding by the cars on either side of us without pause. Each time, raucous cheering from my passengers rewarded me. I knew it was dumb, but I felt like a god.

If I were allowed to freeze parts of an evening, thaw them out, and relive them later, the drive to the cinema on that Wednesday night in January would be on the list.

Ellie patted my shoulder. "Your finest ride by a long shot." I glanced at her and she smiled at me. My chest expanded, filling me with helium and lifting me to the roof.

"Perfect ten?" I asked. *Rate me. Love me again.*

"Hmm … 9.9999. And here we are," Ellie responded.

I pulled in front of the cinema and handed Jonathan the tickets. "I'll park, you guys get in line."

Blood of Mars wasn't on the same popularity level as *Star Wars* or *Matrix*, but the crowd for the sneak preview was substantial enough that we needed a strategy to secure good seats together.

When I met up with them in line, Ellie took the reins.

"J-Dawg, play up your vulnerability. Say 'Excuse me' to people and run like hell to the front. I'll take the left side, and babe"—she caught herself—"Charlie, you take the right."

"Aye, aye, Captain." I saluted.

She unzipped the inside pocket of her fleece and discreetly handed Jonathan his Nerds. "Your contraband-slash-fuel. When the time is right. Godspeed."

Jonathan didn't need fuel, but he tore open the package and chugged.

"He's been really stressed about next year," Ellie murmured to me.

"About starting eighth? Why?"

"Because he's probably starting ninth instead, remember? He likes the idea of skipping ahead, but he's terrified he won't find a group to run with. That's why I was talking to Fred the night of the party; I need him to help get Jonathan into Debate. In fact, they're hanging out tomorrow morning at school so Jonathan can meet some lincoln-douglases before next year."

I swallowed, aware again how insane I must have looked that night, accusing her of dating Fred when she was just trying to look out for her brother.

"They'd be stupid not to take him," I said.

Jonathan stared at us. Ellie pulled me aside and said in a lower voice, "Jonathan thinks no one will want a thirteen-year-old in their group. He thinks he'll be stuck without anyone to protect him."

Her smile was sad. It was useless for her to ask me to help the kid; he wasn't built for sports. We slipped into silence. The line behind us snaked around the side of the building. Five minutes until liftoff.

"So how was the choir showdown at the luxurious Pomona Hilton over New Year's?" I said.

"It was okay."

"I heard *West Side Story* Maria almost wrested control from *Sound of Music* Maria," I said. "What happened?"

"Besides our usual whipped-cream fights in the hotel room?"

"Don't tease," I said, and grinned.

"Yeah, they had a falling out. Again. They've been competing for the spring solo, but I think it was more than just a résumé race. They've been at each other's throats about something, but no one really knows what. At least, I don't. I thought they made up at the party on Sunday, though. They seemed closer, or whatever."

"How do you mean?"

She half shrugged. "If you'd been there later on, you'd know what I mean."

I decided not to push. I didn't really want her thinking too much about my behavior at the party.

"Bridget didn't seem too torn up about the overdose. Like she thought *West Side Story* Maria deserved it or something," I said.

"In case you hadn't noticed, Bridget's kind of a sociopath," said Ellie.

"You are correct," I said.

"I tell you one thing . . . of all the girls likely to overdose on anything, let alone acid, *West Side Story* Maria was the last on the list. It wasn't like her at all."

"Her parents and the sheriff's department think someone forced her."

"Has to be. But when? We were within sight of each other all night. She started acting loopy when I left, but before that everyone was having fun, playing stupid party games. Why so many questions, detective?"

"I keep thinking—the last thing she saw before the hospital was the inside of my car. It was part of her night—it's this weird connection between us. I want to know what happened to her."

Time was up.

We reached the ticket taker, secured our stubs, and split up, dashing in our respective directions.

Jonathan managed to grab three seats about two-thirds of the way down, a little closer than I would've liked, just off center, but still good, considering. He spread his arms crucifixion style to protect the seats on both sides of him, but that wouldn't do. I wanted to sit next to Ellie.

Ellie and I reached him from opposite directions at about the same time and exchanged high fives over his head.

Jonathan's gaze was locked, in increasing horror, on the tall man coming up the aisle in the row ahead of us. "No, no, no," he whispered. There was no escape now; people had filled in all the spots surrounding us.

If this dude sat in front of Jonathan, he would block Jonathan's view of the entire screen. Frack, he'd block *anyone's* view. I acted quickly, dipping down and pouring half my bottled water on the seat in front of Ellie.

"Charlie!" she cried.

The tall man reached the "ruined" seat. "Oh my gosh, watch out, don't sit there," I said, dripping with concern for my fellow man. "Someone spilled soda on it."

He looked at me, surprised by my generosity. "Wow, thanks." He moved one more seat.

I pulled Jonathan behind the now-empty one. "Best seat in the house."

Jonathan smiled. He was probably the only person in the theater with an unencumbered view.

"And I'll take this one," I said, seating myself behind Tall Guy, and next to Ellie.

"Are you sure?" she asked. "Because I don't care about the movie."

"So why'd you come?"

She looked lost, and a bit upset. "I don't know. Let me pay you back for our tickets."

"No, I wanted to treat you guys. I promised Jonathan a long time ago . . ."

"I'm not sure I can do this," she said, fiddling with her hands.

I gently pulled them into mine. "Do what?"

"Be with you, and not be *with* you. If I have fun tonight, I'll want to get back together, and I don't know if that's the right thing for us."

"Like, as individuals on some kind of path?" I said, rolling my eyes.

"I thought it would hurt less to break up now rather than later. I was wrong."

"So you were going to break up with me at the end of the year no matter what?" I said, my voice rising. Did it always come back to graduation and college? Where the fuck had she applied that it would be impossible to stay together?

"No! No—that's not what I meant."

"Then what did you mean?"

"A lot of people drift apart after high school, Charlie. I'm not saying we would have for sure, but—it must have crossed your mind, too?"

Of course it had. It had crossed my mind since our *first date*. Before we'd even said good night, I was trying to figure out how I would possibly hold on to her.

"It's just one movie," I said, monotone. "Your brother's with us."

She insisted on giving me a twenty-dollar bill. I closed my hand around hers.

The first preview started. I couldn't see shit and I didn't care. I focused all my attention on Ellie's hand. The movie was only eighty-three minutes, and the one review I'd read said even that was too long.

"How come we almost never went to the movies when we were dating?" I whispered.

"Because you don't talk if you go to the movies. You just sit there, zoned out."

TV bored Ellie, and most films annoyed her. She only liked weird films or foreign films. It didn't have to be good, it just had to be unpredictable. The rare times we'd watched TV at my house or her house, it was with the volume down so we could do all the character voices ourselves. *"What you say will be more interesting,"* she told me once.

She was always delighted when I found some obscure listing in the paper; she liked crashing meetings for documentary screenings, free art shows, or strange political party offshoots. It was a game, a challenge, to take her to things no one else our age would care about doing, like visiting the Exotic Feline Conservation Center in Rosamond.

Mom once found me in the kitchen at one in the morning in a panic, flipping through the newspaper's arts section, looking for something cool to do with Ellie on our date. Mom urged me to go to bed, said it "shouldn't be so hard," and that if Ellie cared more about what we did than whom she was with, it wasn't fair to me. Over breakfast, having clearly been briefed by my mother on the situation, Dad chimed in, "When you're with the right person, you could go grocery shopping and it would still be fun."

What they didn't understand was the rush I felt when I'd successfully surprised Ellie; the smile she wore just for me. (And seriously, when's the last time Mom and Dad frolicked through the frozen-food aisle together?)

"There's something nice about not being able to talk during a movie, though."

I caressed her fingertips in tiny circles, one by one. I traced patterns on her palm, wanting her to know her fortunes belonged to me, included me. I was going to make her remember exactly how good I could be.

After about fifteen minutes of all my best moves, she leaned over and licked my ear. It was just a tiny swipe along the shell, but it drove me crazy.

"I don't want this to be our last date," she whispered, and her breath was cool and shivery along my skin where she'd licked me.

I'm so thirsty, I wanted to whisper back.

We fumbled our way out of our seats and out of the theater into the lobby. I pushed her against the wall and kissed her neck, working my way up the smooth column of her throat, along her jaw, across her cheek, and finally to her lips. She clutched my hair, encouraging me to go harder, faster, higher. I flashed through a dozen memories of making out with her in the days and weeks and months past, in the school hallway ("Get a room," people griped, oh so originally), in my car, in her bedroom, on the floor, on the couch, and then I stopped and forced myself to focus on this moment, this reality, which was a thousand times better than anything last fall because it was happening *now*; she was making soft moans I almost couldn't hear, so soft they were more like vibrations under the surface. She clutched my arms, either pushing me away or pulling me in; I wasn't sure.

"Damn," Ellie murmured when we came up for air. "You know that thing I was afraid of? It's happening."

My fingers traced the skin just under her shirt at the waistband of her jeans. Her lips were red from the force of my kisses. It was way prettier than any waxy lipstick could ever be.

We reluctantly walked back inside the theater.

When the movie ended, we stood in the lobby again, feeling awkward around each other. Jonathan exited the bathroom and looked at the big clock on the wall above the movie schedule. "It's still early. Can we see it again?"

"But it's not a surprise anymore; you already know the twists and turns. It'll pale in comparison," said Ellie.

"No it won't!"

"You know why you want to see it again? Because you want to feel the way you felt the first time, before you knew what would happen." She looked right at me as she said this. "You don't care about the movie—you care about how you felt, when it was new."

"Sometimes it's better the second time around," I offered, grasping at straws. Had I lost her again, before I'd really gotten her back?

"I just want to see the car go off the bridge one more time," said Jonathan, looking between us like we were crazy. "But whatever, maybe someone'll post it to YouTube."

We pulled up to my house, and I didn't want to try to mack in front of the kid so I squeezed Ellie's hand, and said, "Give me a second with J-dawg?"

I opened the car door for him and motioned for him to follow me a few feet away.

I knew exactly how I was going to get the flash drive out tomorrow. The best part was, Ellie would help me.

I handed Jonathan the twenty dollars she'd given me: re-distribution of wealth. "I need you to swipe Ellie's jacket tonight, the fleece she's wearing now, and take it to the high school tomorrow morning for your meeting with Fred. When you're done, drop it in the lost and found."

"Why?"

"It's kind of a secret, but I'll explain later. Do you accept the mission?"

He smiled. "Accepted."

We shook hands, and I knew I could trust him. Or at least my twenty dollars could.

They drove away, and I walked to my front door. My footsteps triggered the porch light, revealing Ryder curled up in a ball beside the creosote bushes. He had a black eye and a blood-smeared mouth, and he looked about two seconds away from passing out.

THE TRUTH ABOUT RYDER

I HELPED RYDER UP AND LED HIM INTO THE HOUSE. HE weighed a ton. His arm was like an anchor around my neck, dragging me down. We half wobbled, half crawled to the living room couch.

Mom gave him a frozen bag of peas for his eye, some water, and a couple Tylenol. She wanted to call the sheriff's department, but Ryder begged her not to, so she didn't; no judgment, no questions asked.

Mom always had a soft spot for Ryder. It was almost like she respected him for surviving his life, respected his ability to withstand circumstances her own son would never have to worry about. She'd never let me get away with the things Ryder did, because she knew I'd never be forced to do them, and I think a small part of her disliked me for it.

We all agreed he should spend the night.

I put a pot of coffee on.

Ryder looked worse in the accusatory light of the kitchen; accusatory toward *me*, in particular. I had a feeling this night had been a long time coming, and just because I'd preferred to avoid it, and just because I'd sworn up and down to Ellie that Ryder was a good guy, didn't mean I didn't know something was seriously wrong and had been since freshman year. The light in the kitchen was about to reveal all and I couldn't close my eyes against it.

His face had been bludgeoned, and his nose looked like it'd been moved half an inch to the left. Dried blood matted down his hair, sticking it in strands to his neck. It made me think of an animal I'd seen on the freeway, struggling to make it to the side of the road after being hit by a car.

"What happened?" I said, once Mom stopped helicoptering and left for her bedroom, telling us to call her if we needed anything.

"If you couldn't unlock the window tonight, all you had to do was let me know." His voice was low and his words were garbled, as though he had rocks in his mouth.

Jesus. "I'm sorry, man. I just forgot. I completely forgot."

"Whatever. I'm only here to find out about the soccer game, then I'll go," Ryder told me. He sounded slow and clogged, like he had a cold, but worse. Maybe blood and snot had mixed up there.

His face was painful to look at. Even though I was afraid of the answer, I asked, "Who did this to you?" but he didn't reply. Maybe that's why I'd asked; I knew he wouldn't tell me, and then I wouldn't have to do anything about it.

I opened my wallet. "Here, at least take back your cash. I'm really sorry, man."

Ryder scoffed at the money, knocking it out of my hands. "Don't be sorry. Just tell me what the deal is," he said. "I need to know what's going down on Friday. Right now."

"I can't throw the game," I said.

He shifted uncomfortably. "Don't show up. No one will question it. You've been skipping practice, you've been sick, just stay home on Friday. Everyone knows you're drunk half the time, anyway."

"Not anymore."

His eyebrows lifted and he winced, raising his hand and a sodden piece of tissue to lightly touch the swollen area around his eye.

"That coffee's not spiked with whiskey?" he asked.

I handed it over. He took a sip; frowned.

"Ellie wants me to stop drinking," I explained.

He handed the cup back. "That's my Charlie. His moral compass always points E."

I swallowed, unsure if I felt embarrassed or angry. "Lay off, all right? I said I was sorry about the window, and I'm giving you your money back, but I can't throw the game. What's with you lately?"

He laughed, a hollow, bitter sound. It was the laugh of someone who was empty inside and could only mimic sounds instead of create them; could only conjure up the opposite of what a laugh should be, because it had been so long since he'd experienced real joy or humor. " 'Lately'? Now you ask? 'Lately,' he says."

The day after Ryder threw the bat, we'd had nowhere to go, so we kicked an old soccer ball around. We spent the rest of the summer practicing and reading all my dad's *X-Men* comics. Ryder had remembered what I'd said about Lockheed that first day of practice, and he wanted to find out more.

Turns out I was good at soccer, but I never would have known if Ryder hadn't sabotaged Little League for himself. He could've gone far, maybe even pro ball. The minor leagues? Maybe even the majors? Who knows?

He always acted like it didn't matter, but his sacrifice had saved me.

I paced back and forth around the kitchen table, let the words I'd been suppressing for years pour out of me, unfiltered.

"Look—you should've been on the soccer team with me. You should've been on soccer or baseball or football. Hell, I don't know—any team you wanted. And then you wouldn't be betting from the sidelines. You'd be the one deciding if we won or lost, the one getting a scholarship to leave Palm Valley behind. It should've been *you* playing all these years and you *know* that—"

"Yeah, well, that wasn't an option." He got up and slowly, painfully walked toward the door. "Have a beautiful life, Charlie."

I moved to catch up with him.

"You can't even walk straight. Where are you gonna go? Crash here tonight, get some rest. Tell me what's going on, man."

He reached a hand out to the wall to steady himself; turned to face me. "You know Griffin hates you, right? That he always has?"

"He's the one who cut my brakes when I was twelve, isn't he?" I said. "Egged the house? Crank-called us?"

Ryder nodded shortly. "I mean, I don't know if he did *all* those things. But he blames you for ruining our lives. Thinks if you hadn't moved here, Mom would still have a job at the school, we'd still have our old house, and Dad wouldn't be in prison." He laughed again, the sound like an off-key piano. "Like you guys *made* him rip off Flynn Scientific! Like you *made* him sell stolen auto parts! It's lame, but that's what Griffin thinks. He promised to leave you alone if I helped him on his deliveries, served as a scout."

"Why'd you fail the drug test freshman year?" I blurted out.

"*I wasn't on drugs*," said Ryder. "I mean, I wasn't taking them for myself. He forced me to test the product every once in a while, make sure it wasn't bad."

I thought I might be sick. "That's horrible." I wish I'd known, back then. But what could I have done about it? I remembered Ryder being summoned yesterday by Griffin and Griffin's friend. "*The nose knows.*" A cocaine sample to test?

Ryder wobbled back into the living room and sat down on the couch.

"After I failed the test, and I couldn't be on any of the teams, I had nowhere to go, no group to join; everywhere was a slammed door. I told Griffin I was done with him, but I was getting my ass kicked all the time at school, so it was like . . . my only way out was through him. He and his friends said they'd protect me if I started working for them again. It's screwed up, but there it is."

"What kind of drugs did they make you take?" I asked.

"Mostly it was coke," Ryder said. "Occasionally weed, if the grower changed. I didn't mind the weed so much. But tonight, it was supposed to be LSD. After what happened to Maria, I said 'Hell, no.' She might've overdosed, or it might've been a bad batch—Griffin doesn't really know what he's doing; it's all an experiment for him. I wasn't gonna take that risk, so I refused, and I fought him off and I ran here."

I wiped a hand down my face. "He's the one who drove my car to the hospital, isn't he? Tried to make it look like I dosed Maria Salvador?"

Ryder hesitated. "Yeah. If Salvador died, and word got around, his business would go with her; no one would buy from him anymore. He's trying to expand through Agua Dulce down to the San Fernando Valley, the edge of Van Nuys."

"Since when do songbirds do drugs?"

"Posey asked me for LSD. Said she was going to teach the Other Maria a lesson, trick her into taking it."

"She wanted her out of commission so she could have the concert solo," I muttered.

"Whatever her reasons were, I didn't care. I know what it's like to be force-fed, so that was off the table."

"That's when she called you a cylon?"

"We had a fight and I left. That's when you saw me at the party, on my way out the door. I think after that, Bridget must've called Griffin, and he came over to make the deal. Bridget is, like, Posey's henchman."

Bridget always told me I was too nice, too bland, too sweet.

Had she found what she was looking for in Ryder's older brother?

"We were gone by the time he must've showed up," I said. "Bridget dropped me off at home by nine."

As I said the words, something clicked into place for me. She hadn't been my alibi. *I'd been hers.*

"So Griffin probably sold it to Posey and stuck around, maybe to see if any high school girls would hook up. And when things got bad, he used your car to drop Salvador off at the hospital," Ryder theorized.

"Hold on. Ellie said the Marias made up, though," I pointed out. "They were getting along at the party. I think Posey changed her mind. I don't think she dosed Salvador after all."

If it wasn't *Sound of Music* Maria who'd slipped her the huge amount of LSD, who was it? When did they do it? And why?

"We have to tell the sheriff's department about Griffin, what he's been doing, what he's been making you do," I said.

Ryder looked away and let his head swivel around on a kind of figure-eight track. "No, man, I don't know . . . If Griffin found out I squealed, this'll be a pleasant memory." He pointed to his face.

"Stay here tonight, and we'll go in the morning; I have to go down there anyway to get my car back. We'll tell them everything you told me. They have him on tape dropping her off! They'll arrest him; you'll be free—you'll never have to do any of this shit again."

A brief spark of hope ignited in his good eye. "The reason I asked you to throw the game . . ."

"It's okay, I get it now. You *had* to get out of here."

"It wasn't so I could make money. I mean, it was, but it wasn't just that. It was so I could nail Griffin. He's betting you'll win."

I flashed on Griffin at the trailer, grinning his sick grin at me and whispering, "Go get 'em, killer."

"He thinks you're on his side. Thinks I brought you over yesterday to make sure you did everything you could to win. He doesn't know I have my own bet going. I want him to lose big, put a dent in his cash flow, so he'll have to cool it for a while."

I looked at Ryder and I didn't see a beaten young man, desperate and half ruined; I saw him as a kid, strong and proud and defiant in the summer sun, throwing his bat against the chain-link fence. That kid was still in there somewhere, and I had to help him.

"I get it," I said. "This'll all be over tomorrow."

THE SHORT ARM OF THE LAW

MOM MADE US WAFFLES FOR BREAKFAST. ON RYDER'S WAFFLE, she placed a chocolate chip in each minisquare, the way she used to when we were kids. When he smiled at her, it was more like a wince that traveled up his face to squeeze the pain out of his black eye.

As an afterthought, Mom asked if I wanted chocolate chips on my waffle, too.

I opted for a box of Total. When my mom was growing up, her parents had no money, so the only thing she and her sisters got for Christmas were common grocery store items, like a variety pack of twenty small boxes of sweet cereal (Froot Loops, Lucky Charms). After they ate the cereal, they kept the boxes and played "grocery store checkout" with them.

When my mom looks at Ryder, I think she sees those Christmas days, the idea of going without and emerging tougher and leaner. She learned to cherish the kinds of things her classmates threw away.

I think she really believed the work she did with Fresh Start was supposed to level the playing field—give every student a fairer shot. And maybe it would have if Ryder hadn't failed the drug test, and if Ryder wasn't, in fact, stealing Mr. Donovan's test questions to tilt the scores in favor of the kids who could pay for them.

I consoled myself with the thought that soon Ryder wouldn't have to do that anymore. With Griffin locked up, he wouldn't need to make money to escape—he could just live his life. But what kind of life would he have at this point?

Dad wasn't scheduled to teach his New Media journalism class until ten on Thursday mornings, so he took us to the sheriff's department before school. I marched up to the counter and requested an audience with Deputy Thompson, our private protection service all those summers ago when we first moved to town.

From that point on, nothing happened the way I expected it to.

Turned out the deputies had tangled with Ryder before.

"You catch him breaking and entering?" said Thompson, walking up to my dad and ignoring me and Ryder completely.

"What? No!" I said. "That's not why we're here."

"I knew this was a bad idea," muttered Ryder, looking ready to rabbit.

Thompson didn't even glance at us. He was immobile, a brick wall, waiting for Dad to reply.

"Absolutely not," said Dad firmly. "We've never had problems with Ryder. He's an old family friend, and he's in trouble, and we came here for help. Is that a problem?"

"No problem at all," said Thompson unconvincingly. "Come on back." He led us to a private room with no windows, just a long table and a landline phone. Dad and I happened to take our seats on one side of the table, with Ryder on the other. I immediately regretted it; now it looked like we *had* brought him in for questioning. But Thompson sat next to Ryder before I could get up and move.

"All right, what's this about?"

We went over Griffin's history of dealing and forcing Ryder to be the guinea pig. I filled in the blanks whenever Ryder faltered. Thompson took notes on a legal pad.

"These are pretty serious allegations," he said, turning to face Ryder at last. "What made you come to us now? Trying to get out of your own mess by turning your brother in?"

"No, I'm not—I'm just sick of it. I want out."

"Can you help us or not?" I said. Dad gave me a look, but I let it bounce off me.

"I'd like to, but as far as Charlie's car, we haven't been able to lift any prints, certainly none that match Griffin's. I believe you're telling the truth, or part of the truth, but we have nothing to hold him on. Unless you want to press charges for that?" He motioned to Ryder's black eye.

Ryder looked at Thompson like he was crazy. "He'll deny it, and the most you can do is hold him for, what, seventy-two hours?"

"We handed you Griffin on a platter, and you're not going to do anything?" I sputtered, standing up and slamming my hand on the table.

"I knew it," said Ryder, standing as well, his eyes darting anxiously, looking around like Griffin was about to show up and finish the pummeling he'd started the night before.

"Wait, hold on," said Dad. "The other deputy told us about a baseball cap, how the driver caught on tape was wearing a Flynn Scientific cap. Charlie saw Griffin wearing it."

"Circumstantial," said Thompson. "Hey, I wish I had a better answer for you, and I appreciate you coming down here, but we can't move on this information without something more concrete than a vengeful little brother's testimony. A vengeful little brother with priors of his own."

"Thanks for serving and protecting. Truly. I think I might be tearing up at your dedication to this community," I said.

"Charlie—"

"This is bullshit, Dad, and you know it."

"Arguing and making smart-ass remarks isn't going to help your cause. I think—"

"What if . . . ," said Ryder quietly, his Adam's apple bobbing nervously. We all leaned forward to hear. "The next buy is two days from now. Saturday night. I can tell you the time and location and you can see it all for yourself."

"On Saturday nights most of my men are stationed at check points for DUIs, but I'll see what I can do."

It didn't sound very promising.

"I'm in," I told Ryder the second we were outside, waiting for the deputies to pull my car around and release Amelia back to my custody. Dad had already left for work.

"What do you mean?" Ryder asked.

"I'm in. The soccer match. Whatever you need me to do. I'll give Steve three penalty kicks if that's what it takes. We have to bankrupt Griffin."

"*We* don't have to do anything. This is my problem, not yours."

"I want to help."

He told me the spread, the money on the line, and what the different scores and outcomes would mean. Griffin had bet that Palm Valley would either win or tie. Ryder had bet that Agua Dulce would win flat-out. If Agua Dulce won by any amount, Ryder stood to make three grand and Griffin stood to lose one. If Agua Dulce won by two goals or more, Griffin stood to lose three.

I had to make sure we lost, preferably by two goals.

Amelia had never looked worse and had never felt better. Her fender was scratched and she still had white fingerprint dust all over the wheel and dash, but she ran like a dream. Autonomous again, I dropped Ryder back at my house so he could recuperate some more, and I took off for school.

It was time for Phase Two of my plan to break into the principal's office.

LIBERATING THE FLASH DRIVE

THERE WERE THREE WAYS TO GET SENT TO THE PRINCIPAL'S office:

1. Pick a fight
2. Sass a teacher
3. Cause a public disturbance

To expedite the mission I went for all three.

As I pulled into the parking lot at Palm Valley High, I received confirmation from Jonathan that he'd completed his end of the heist. Ellie's jacket was planted in lost and found.

"Bammity bam," his text said. I guess the new generation had their own lingo. Or maybe it was just Jonathan being weird.

In second period, I made sure to sit behind the infamous Fred, lincoln-douglas extraordinaire, he of Ellie's bad macking session at the party on Sunday. I was going to enjoy this part.

"Yo, Fred-day," I said, five minutes before class ended. "Did you hit on my girl at Maria Posey's party?"

"What? Um—no—I thought—"

I kicked out the legs of his desk, with him in it, and he went sprawling.

"Charlie Dixon, what was that?" Ms. Daniels roared. "Sit back in your chair."

That was it? What did it take to get sent to the principal's office these days? Short shorts and a crop top baring my belly button? I had to step up my game.

When Fred staggered to his feet, I whacked him in the midsection with my textbook like I was golfing. He doubled over, shocked and furious.

"Charlie, what's gotten into you?" Ms. Daniels sputtered.

I held my hands up. "You should've heard what he just called you. I won't repeat it because we're in mixed company, but wow."

"What?" Fred gasped. "I didn't say anything!"

"I mean, I could come up and write it on the board, but I think we'd all be suspended just for looking at it. In fact, I'm not even sure I *understand* it—"

"He's lying! I don't really even know any bad words!" said Fred. "On the debate team, we argue eloquently."

I should've hit him in the mouth.

"It starts with the letter C," I said.

Fred tried to swipe at me, but I dodged him.

"Both of you are getting Cs for the day. I mean, Fs!" Ms. Daniels said, flustered. "Go to Principal Jeffries's office, now."

I scooped up my backpack and skipped down the hall, urging Fred to follow suit. "Time's a-wastin', hurry it up now."

"What's wrong with you?" he cried. "I didn't say anything about Ms. Daniels, and as far as Ellie—"

I stopped in my tracks and turned around. Fred took a step back, even though we had almost a full hallway length between us.

"Don't even think her name, let alone say it."

"It was just spin the friggin' bottle," he protested. "Everyone was playing. I'm surprised you didn't hear about the beckham drama. Delinsky kissed Patrick's girlfriend, Josh kissed Delinksy's chick, the Marias kissed, some dot-govs showed up at the last second, even Thomas' English Muffin was playing. Trust me, I wasn't thinking much about Ellie."

I'm only human. I had to take a moment. "The Marias kissed?"

"It was only like time stopped, but yeah, sorry for kissing your *ex*-girlfriend for two seconds." He rolled his eyes.

That's what Ellie meant when she said, "*They made up at the party. If you'd been there, you'd understand.*" They'd kissed! They hadn't just made up, they'd made out. Were the Marias in love with each other? Was that why they fought all the time? Did Ryder know? It gave new meaning to the phrase *at each other's throats*.

But there was no time to ponder the intricacies of down-low relationships. I had a mission to fulfill.

"Look, just shut up and follow my lead," I said, praying that Danny had relayed my message to the drama kids in time.

I shoved open the doors to the principal's office.

"Hi, Mrs. Batiglio, we met the other day? This is Fred, he's like a major loose cannon, and I got caught in his path of destruction."

The bell rang. Second period was over—six minutes till third began. When the bell stopped blaring, a trumpet took its place from somewhere outside the office, gaining volume as it approached us.

It was better than I could've dreamed.

Nine members of the marching band, in formation, three by three, followed by the entire drama club, all four years, called for my head on a pike.

Charlie Dixon, you will fall!
An attack on one is an attack on all!

The drama kids, those beautiful egomaniacs, had recruited the marching band to humiliate me: a trumpeter, cymbals crasher, drums, tuba, and clarinet. It was the ugliest "song" I ever heard, but it did the trick.

I'd figured I'd get an aria, like the time Will Norris, then a senior playing Romeo, stole a kiss offstage from the freshman girl playing Juliet. A huge etiquette breach. They serenaded him for weeks, rhyming "cradle robber" with "fishmonger," which was apparently some kind of Shakespearean insult.

My punishment may have lacked finesse, but the distraction worked. The chant took hold and rocked the hallway as the group clogged up every corridor.

Charlie Dixon, you will fall!
An attack on one is an attack on all!

The old bat didn't know who or what to look at, which was the whole point of the distraction. Principal Jeffries came outside to check on the commotion, too.

In the chaos, I dove under Jeffries's desk and dug through the lost-and-found box. I found the flash drive (which had a sticker of a cartoon character, black, white, and yellow, with four points on its head. I had no idea what the frack it was; if I'd had a hundred years to guess, I wouldn't have come close to guessing it), scrabbled to open Ellie's fleece jacket, and slipped the flash drive inside her inner pocket, the way she'd smuggled Nerds into the movies last night. I zipped it closed and stuffed it back in the box just as Jeffries's feet appeared in my view.

"What are you doing?" said Principal Jeffries.

"Dropped my pens," I said, standing and straightening up, and showing him a fistful. He winced, and pushed the lost-and-found box farther under his desk.

"Come into the other room, please." He squinted suspiciously at me and locked the door behind him.

I bobbed my head to the cadence of the march, which was still going on outside. It was sort of catchy. And Danny would be a hero among the art, drama, and band kids for setting it up.

"I misunderstood Fred," I said. "It's all on me. I thought he called Ms. Daniels an extremely naughty word. Turns out he called her a Bundt cake." I smacked my forehead. "Inappropriate, sure. But also kind of flattering. For a woman her age. Don't Bundt cakes have nice curves or something?"

Mr. Jeffries and Mrs. Batiglio stared at me.

Civilizations died and were reborn.

"You feel the need to defend the fairer sex, is that it?" Jeffries said. "You like to think of yourself as chivalrous. The last time I saw you in this office you had destroyed another student's property."

"Right. All due respect, sir, the camera lens was pointed up. Through female legs."

"Carl claims he was documenting the staircase's water damage from the storm the night before."

"I scrolled through the pictures before I took action, and the only thing damp was—"

"That's enough! That's two strikes this school year, Mr. Dixon. Three strikes and you're out of soccer. I wouldn't want that, not with tomorrow's game coming up." He cleared his throat. "Think you'll win against Agua Dulce?"

Jesus, had he placed a bet, too? And was he for or against us?

Mrs. Batiglio rolled her eyes. *Men.*

The rest of the school day I expected to be ambushed by Bridget's partner in crime, hoping it wouldn't be Griffin but knowing, deep down, that it probably was.

I took corners cautiously; I opened my locker slowly; and I sat in the back row in all my classes so no one could sneak up behind me.

I knew I wouldn't be allowed to leave school grounds without someone paying me a not-so-friendly visit. That's why the flash drive was going to be safely carried off campus by Ellie instead, tipped off by now by her brother.

I made it out to the soccer field just in time for Coach to announce a new lineup for Friday's game. Josh and I would both be starting. Josh didn't look at me, but I saw a smirk lift the corner of his lip like an invisible fishhook, and stinking just as much.

It was tough to concentrate on drills. I kept wondering if Ellie had made it home with her jacket okay. After practice, I showered and changed, intending to head straight to Ellie's and fill her in.

However, someone else had other plans for me. He was waiting for me by my car, and he didn't look happy.

BRIDGET'S SILENT PARTNER

"MR. DONOVAN?"

"Charlie. We need to talk."

He placed a hand on my shoulder, and I removed it.

"About what?"

"I think you know what, Charlie."

I wasn't crazy about the way he kept saying my name. It wasn't like Maria Posey, who acted like she needed a hazmat suit around me, but it was . . . overly familiar. Like Mr. D. and I were old pals who joked around in history class, like we had that special student-teacher relationship that only comes around every couple of years. Please. I had nothing against the guy, but I had nothing for him, either.

I thought he was a dupe for not picking up on Ryder's scheme, for believing he was such a gosh-darn inventive teacher that his lessons made a difference in our lives and test scores.

"Suppose you fill me in anyway," I said. "Pretend I don't know, and we'll go from there."

"Bridget and I had an arrangement, and she told me you and she had an arrangement. That means we're on the same side."

It sounded more like a triangle trying to eat itself.

I didn't like being seen after school chatting up a teacher in the parking lot, but I wasn't about to invite him inside my car. Amelia would never forgive me for getting the stench of faculty on her upholstery.

Besides, he was tall, balding, and slight, with wire-rimmed glasses and small hands. I could take him in a fight, no question; I could wipe the floor with his elbow-patch tweed jacket if need be.

"What exactly did Bridget tell you? Because I have it on good authority she lies," I said.

"Cut the crap, Charlie. Just give me the flash drive. It doesn't belong to you, and you have no right to it. A lot of people are going to be affected, some close to home, and I don't think you've thought this through."

Holy puke. *Was* it naked photos of Bridget after all? Had Mr. Donovan snapped them?

I shrugged. "I don't have the flash drive."

A campus security guard appeared on the horizon, walking toward us.

"I'm going to have to ask you to empty your backpack and pockets," said Mr. Donovan, stepping aside to give me room.

"Everything okay?" said the guard.

"We're about to find out," said Mr. Donovan. "I've asked Charlie to comply with a quick search. Several students have come to me with rumors that he's carrying a switchblade."

"A switchblade, really?" I said incredulously. "Is it for the rumble this weekend? Why not a broadsword or nunchucks?"

"Well, those wouldn't fit in your backpack, would they, son?" asked the guard. "Empty your backpack, please."

Burning, I unzipped my bag and shook it out. Itchy and Scratchy went through each of the bag's pockets and slid their hands through the lining, too. Then they made me empty my jean pockets.

"Are we done here? Am I free to go?" I asked, gathering my notebooks and pencils and shoving them back into my bag.

Mr. Donovan dismissed the security guard to finish his rounds and then sat down beside me as I cleaned up their mess.

"I'm sorry," he said, sounding weary and defeated. He took off his glasses and rubbed his eyes. "I shouldn't have done that. It's just—I'm certain if you understood the ramifications of your actions, you'd behave differently. I care about this school. I care about my debate team. I don't know what they'd— It's been too much, these last couple of years, too much to ask of them, and of me. But they deserve to succeed."

"Do you have, like, a therapist you can talk to?" I said. "Because midlife crises aren't my forte."

I left him sitting there, alone in the school parking lot, his face in his hands, as I drove away.

THE ANGRY PENGUIN

I DIDN'T HAVE TO DRIVE ALL THE WAY TO ELLIE'S TO TALK TO
her. She was walking her neighbor's decrepit red Labrador on
Antelope Drive, halfway between Palm Valley High and her house.

"Walking" was a generous term; Ellie practically had to drag the
old dog along on his leash. He kept trying to sit. I knew how he felt.
It was that kind of day.

The pooch's real name: Freckles. His temporary name while
in Ellie's care, which she swore fit him better and afforded him a
higher degree of dignity: Mr. Melanin.

I pulled over slowly so I wouldn't startle her. "Freckles looks
beat. Hop in."

"*Mr. Melanin* needs the exercise. And I need the less-than-
minimum wage."

I shut my car engine off and joined Ellie outside. The dog
wagged its tail at me.

"Hi, boy," I said, patting him on the head. "What's that, boy? You
want a less cancery name?"

Ellie refused to take the bait. "I heard the drama kids nailed you
with a free-range marching band after second period. How you
holding up?"

"Pretty good, considering I orchestrated the whole thing," I said, and winked at her.

"Sure you did," she teased. "Who wouldn't want a personalized marching song written and dedicated to their bullying ways?"

"Moi? I'm no bully. It was all part of my plan."

Thus we entered Phase Three: reel in Ellie as a full partner.

"I needed a distraction in the hallway so I could steal something out of the principal's office," I added casually.

She gave me her full attention now. "What?"

As we towed our reluctant canine captive up the road, I told her everything that'd happened since Monday. How Bridget had approached me in the library intending to blackmail me but realized you catch more flies with honey; how I'd IM'd with a mysterious entity going by the initials BM; how BM had offered me cash for the drive, and assumed I'd been hired by a girl other than Bridget; how I'd discovered the drive in lost and found but had no way of freeing it; and, last, how Mr. Donovan had practically begged me for the flash drive today after practice.

"Jeez, Charlie. You've been busy. And you still had time to chat me up every night and take me to the movies? I'm flattered."

"I combined objectives," I admitted.

"How so?"

"You tell me."

"I'm lost," she said. "Does that mean you have the flash drive?"

"In a manner of speaking." I couldn't stop smiling. I'd been waiting all day for this moment.

Ellie tapped her foot impatiently. "Well, what's on it?"

"No idea."

"There's cryptic, and then there's annoying."

"Check the inner pocket of your jacket," I said.

She did.

Freckles had never been dragged around the block faster.

In the safety of Ellie's bedroom, we fired up Ellie's laptop and prepared to gaze upon the flash drive's contents. Jonathan was hanging around outside, wanting to know what we were up to.

I wasn't in the mood to humor him, but I did my best. "Hey, buddy, can you give us some time alone?" I knew I was being condescending, but Jonathan didn't. He thought I sounded kind. What bothered me about the situation was not the disparity between my feelings and behavior but the fear that I was once the recipient of such hypocrisy without knowing it, either; that every time someone had been kind to me as a child, it was with the same wince or cringe or secret desire to get rid of me that I harbored now. Because in Jonathan I saw my old self. My nerdy, comic-book-reading, eager-to-please, chatty little self, who would've gotten eaten alive at a new school if not for the saving grace of Ryder.

Jonathan was so desperate for us to tolerate his company he even offered to make us snacks. We accepted, in the hopes of keeping him out of our way for the next five minutes.

"Why does the flash drive have a Badtz-Maru sticker on it?" said Ellie, once Jonathan was gone.

"You know what that thing is?" I held up the drive and squinted at it.

"Bad Badtz-Maru."

"What's a 'bad Badtz-Maru'?"

"It's a penguin; he's like one of Hello Kitty's underlings."

"How can you tell? It doesn't even remotely look like a penguin."

"It's more a feeling," she laughed. "Anatomical accuracy is not the Sanrio people's strong suit."

"Oh, come on. Hello Kitty is an excellent depiction of a cat with no mouth, tail, claws, or profile."

"There's a store at the mall that sells nothing but cutesy shit. I've seen it in there."

"Is it bored or hostile?" I asked, squinting harder at the sticker.

"I'm pretty sure it's filled with rage. So quit stalling." She took the flash drive from me.

"I made ants on a log," said Jonathan, kneeing the door open and balancing a tray with two plates of celery, peanut butter, and raisins.

Oh boy. It was a fourth grader's idea of a snack. That settled it: he *was* going to get eaten alive in high school next year.

"Great, thanks," said Ellie, showing Jonathan the door. "We'll just be a second."

We couldn't risk him seeing nudie pics on the drive, if indeed that's what it contained. Ellie shut the door on him.

The drive was titled "M. Salvador. Tests." Onscreen was a series of files, labeled by date.

We clicked on a recent one, labeled November 1. It was a grainy photograph of a Scantron test. The bubbles had been filled in with a number two pencil, and Maria Salvador's name was printed neatly at the top.

The document labeled November 3 revealed the same test, graded and returned, an A- circled. Viewed side by side, it was clear the bubbles of the two tests were slightly different. The pattern stuck out to the left or right where once it had been centered.

The test had been tampered with. Corrected.

We clicked on other files, other dates. There were a variety of tests, but most of them were Maria Salvador's. They dated from August through November of last fall. One or two other names cropped up, the images slightly blurred this time, as though Maria had taken the photos at a strange angle, on the sly.

She'd been collecting evidence all year. Every once in a while the tests were the same before and after being turned in, but only if the grade was a B+ or higher.

"How'd she take the photos?" Ellie wondered.

"Cell phone?" I suggested.

"In the middle of class? No way."

"Key chain?" I said. I remembered Maria Salvador clutching a key chain at the hospital, rocking back and forth with it. It was sort of plain and clunky-looking, and she refused to let go of it.

"The Hello Kitty store." Ellie snapped her fingers. "Same place she got the penguin sticker. They sell novelty key chains with cameras. But who's been changing the tests? Another student?"

"Actually, I think it's Mr. Donovan, based on his weird speech to me today."

Ellie groaned and pressed a hand to her forehead. "He's bumping everyone's grades up!"

"Just slightly—just enough to place them in a higher GPA."

"Just enough to keep his job and performance bonuses," she added cynically.

"Just enough to keep funding for the debate team in place," I offered.

"I never had a class with him," Ellie griped. "My loss, apparently."

"Would you really want a GPA boost from him cheating?"

"Everyone else is getting one! *You* are."

"Maybe not. I have a solid B."

"Maybe you have a solid C."

"Hey, it's not like I knew about this! I didn't ask him to do it."

"No, I know. I'm sorry. It's just—"

"And what about your calculus teacher last year? She used to tell you exactly which questions would be on the test. How is that any better?"

"It's not," she agreed after a moment. "But if he's been fixing all the grades since August, probably longer, he's toast. He'll never teach anywhere again. And you know what? Good effing riddance. I've been busting my ass all year when all I had to do was transfer to Donovan's class and let him pave me a golden road straight to the Ivy League—Charlie? Still with me?"

If Donovan was really boosting everyone's scores to keep his job and bonuses in place, his moniker of "best teacher in the school" wasn't because Ryder was selling the test information beforehand; the only cheating going on was *after* the tests were turned in. So what was Ryder doing up there once a week?

"Charlie," said Ellie again, waving her hand in front of my face. "You okay?"

"Yeah. Just thinking."

"You know who we should tell? Your mom. She's the best person to deal with this. She can sort it all out."

"Yeah," I said again, in a daze. "Yeah, you're right."

She kissed me suddenly. My hands lifted up like they had no choice, like the world was upside down and gravity was on the ceiling now. My hands fell upward to cup her face and tangle in her hair. She pulled back just as suddenly.

"Thanks for letting me in on this. I'm glad you told me," she said.

"What are we doing?" I curled my finger around the belt loop of her jeans.

"I don't know," she said simply. "But when we kissed last night at the movies, I couldn't stand thinking we'd never do that again."

"Do you know, the week before we had our first date, I went to every single film at the theater just so I'd know which ones I could safely recommend for us?"

Her shoulders lifted in the smallest of sighs. "And then I told you I didn't want to see a movie. God, I was a bitch."

"No, I liked it."

"You liked that I was a bitch?"

"No, I liked that you didn't want to see a movie. That you didn't want to do what everybody else does."

My mom hadn't shared that view; when I'd told her about the movie fiasco, she'd said, "I hope Ellie's worth it."

"But if I'd known you'd put that much thought into it—"

"I didn't want you to know."

"Did you do that a lot?" she asked.

I swallowed, and feigned confusion. "Do what a lot?"

"Hold back. Only let me see certain things about you, and not everything."

I shrugged, and she looked at me with such sadness, I wondered if I could look at her from now on and *not* see the sadness.

We kissed some more, and I should've been happy, but instead, the same thought kept nagging at me: I was drinking the water, she was mine again. I was quenching my thirst, but it wasn't enough; it would never be enough, not until I could be certain the water would never run out.

I slowed down our kisses, till they were just nibbles, drops in the desert, easing away from her. She made a frustrated sound so I kissed her throat, and then down her shoulders to her arms, to her wrists, and to the tips of her fingers.

"The deadline for Lambert College is tomorrow."

"I know," she said.

"Okay," I said. "And?"

"How many times do we have to talk about this?" she said gently.

"As many times as it takes to get a straight answer."

"Charlie," she said, caressing my face, "I told you I would apply there. *As well as several other schools.* And I meant it. Okay?"

"So you know the deadline's tomorrow."

"Yes," she said.

"If you don't think it's a good enough school, just tell me."

"I've never said that. You're the only one who thinks that. You're the only one giving me motives I don't have, for things I haven't done."

"Well, if you're going to be testy about it . . . ," I teased.

She rolled her eyes. "I have a jewelry portfolio to update, Mister School Conspiracy Uncover-er. Go home and spread the word about Donovan."

But I didn't go home. And I didn't tell my mom. I left the flash drive on Ellie's desk for safekeeping and I told her, "If anyone asks, we're not together, right? And you don't know about the flash drive."

"But we are together." She grinned, leaning in for another kiss.

"Yes, but if anyone asks . . . I don't want you tied to this. I don't want anyone to know that you know," I said seriously. I had some new theories about BM, and I didn't want him threatening Ellie.

"If that's what you want, sure."

We said good-bye and I darted down the stairs. Ellie's mention of having to finish her portfolio reminded me of the reason I'd gotten involved in this mess in the first place.

It was time to pay my dear neighbor a visit.

THE TWO MARIAS

BRIDGET WAS PAINTING HER TOENAILS ON HER BED WHEN I walked in.

"You may as well come clean," I said from the doorway. "I have the flash drive and I've seen what's on it, so now I want to know why. Why you wanted it for yourself."

She set her nail polish aside and flexed her toes. "Guess."

"It's obviously important to Donovan, so maybe you figured you could shake him down for a better grade. But he's already giving people better grades as it is."

"Not bad. Getting warmer."

"But he seems to think you're allies. So maybe the two of you are planning something else."

She smirked. "Now you're getting colder."

"Oh my God, just tell me."

"Why? You didn't come here to give me the drive. I don't owe you a thing."

"No, but I'm open to hearing why you want it and reconsidering who I give it to," I lied.

"How stupid do you think I am, Charlie?"

"You've got nothing to lose at this point."

I picked up her nail polish and cranked open the lid. "Although your bedspread's kind of plain. I think it could use some color." I mimed turning the nail polish over and dumping it across the sheets and comforter.

Bridget sprung forward and snatched the bottle from me. "Whatever. Fine. I'll tell you."

"Start at the beginning."

"I overheard the Marias arguing last Saturday before the state qualifier in Pomona. Maria was *freaking* out, saying how she and Other Maria had a deal; Other Maria was supposed to hand over evidence of Donovan's cheating in exchange for five thousand dollars, pooled together from other classmates."

This seemed worthy of a whistle, so I didn't fight it.

"But Other Maria had a 'change of heart' and decided not to sell it," Bridget continued. "She claimed it wasn't on her anymore; she'd hidden it somewhere at school."

"Why did Maria Posey care so much if Donovan was exposed?"

Bridget gave me a look like I was the biggest moron on the planet. "Think, Dix. If Donovan got fired, and word spread about his little after-school activities, everyone in that class would have to redo history. Colleges would get wind, GPAs would be called into question, and everything coming out of Palm Valley High would be suspect. Scholarships revoked, acceptances overturned, SATs reconsidered. We'd be the Pariah Class of 2014. It'd be a total mess. What's five thousand dollars compared to a semester at Princeton or Barnard? Chump change. *Sound of Music* Maria figures, I'll suppress this info till graduation and get the eff out of Palm Valley. So she made me come up with a plan."

"Made you?"

"She knew I'd overheard, and she made me brainstorm what to do."

"You're her lap dog," I said, disgusted.

"Not anymore," she shot back.

"So what'd you brainstorm?"

"I said lie low, pretend to be friends again, and get *West Side Story* Maria drunk at the celebration on Sunday. Maybe if she's drunk, she'll change her mind and agree to sell the flash drive, or at least confess its location. But if other people were angry, can you blame them? Everyone at that party had something to lose if the information went public. Everyone."

"So you and Griffin aren't dating? You didn't call him up to make a special delivery?"

She looked insulted. "I had *nothing* to do with the LSD, and Griffin doesn't party with high schoolers. If he did show up, it was for a quick and dirty deal. All I knew, when I left with you that night, was that *Sound of Music* Maria was willing to pay at least five thousand for the drive. I figured if I found the drive first, the money would come to me instead."

"The money, and sweet revenge for being her slave the past four years."

"Shut up, Dix, you *got* your first choice. You don't know what it's been like, having to kiss her ass every day."

"Ellie didn't have to do that."

"Ellie doesn't do anything she doesn't want to. Most of us don't have that luxury. Yeah, I wanted revenge. And I knew something she didn't; I'd seen *West Side Story* Maria creeping around the library on Friday."

"Where does Donovan come in? Why'd you clue him in?"

"I realized I could either get the cash from *Sound of Music* Maria or hand the drive to Donovan in exchange for a glowing recommendation letter. Either way I'd be in charge of my own destiny next year, for once. I hadn't decided yet what I was going to do. I was playing it by ear."

"If you're playing it by ear, you're tone-deaf. Your first mistake was getting me on the case."

"I realize that now," she snapped.

"Tell me one more thing," I said.

"What."

"Why'd you forge Ellie's handwriting on that note?"

"Who says it was me?"

Without taking my eyes off her, I reached behind me to her dresser, opened the top drawer, and pulled out a stack of "Ellie's" stationery.

Bridget's eyebrows lifted. "Nice one. How'd you know?"

"Lucky guess."

"My panties are in the next one over."

"Didn't think you wore any."

"Not in the summer," she agreed.

"What was the point in forging it? Did you think that would turn me against her?" I scoffed.

"Hardly," she scoffed back. It was a scoff-a-thon. "It was a test, to see if my handwriting was good enough to pass as hers. If I could get you to believe it was Ellie's, I could use the same handwriting against *Sound of Music* Maria to set up the drop. I couldn't risk her knowing I had the flash drive until she agreed to meet, and agreed to pay me. I wanted her to think it was Ellie up until the moment of the trade."

"Why?"

"I knew you'd protect Ellie, the way you wouldn't protect me."

She sounded hurt, and I had no real answer to that. I didn't bother denying it; that would've insulted us both.

"What about you?" she said. "You claim you have the drive. Congratu-fucking-lations. What'll it be? The cash? Or the honor of destroying a man's career and defunding the debate team while your mom hosts a press conference explaining how her policies ended in scandal?"

"Haven't decided," I growled. "I'm playing it by ear."

Ryder was on his way out when I walked up the driveway to my house. He looked a little steadier on his feet than he had earlier.

"My man," he said, offering his fist for a bump. "Thanks for letting me crash here today. Your mom made me lasagna."

"Where you headed?"

"Finalizing the bets for tomorrow's game. See you then?"

"See you then. Hey, Ryder—quick question."

"Yeah?"

"How do people normally take LSD? Is it like, a pill?"

He looked surprised for a second. "Can be. But usually it's on blotting paper. You have the tray of chemicals, and you dip the paper in, and then cut the paper up into tabs. Why?"

"Just curious. Any other ways?"

"Yeah, you can also use a dropper and place it into food, sugar cubes, or something else. Blotting paper's the best, though, because it cuts down on the amount of additives. Less chance of strychnine or something being added."

I shuddered involuntarily. "Okay. Thanks."

That night for dinner I ate Ryder's leftovers and I watched my parents go about their evening tasks: Organizing the recycling bin. Listening to *Which Way, L.A.?* on NPR. Cracking the windows to get some night air. Turning on the TV for *Flip That House*.

I wondered if Bridget had the right idea about splitting town, even if she just went to UC Irvine.

It hit me like a car flipping over—like that time in the match against Sylmar last year when their midfielder tripped me and I rolled four times after I hit the ground. If Ellie didn't go to school with me, I had to leave. If I stayed here, I would atrophy. My feet would get stuck in the quicksand of Palm Valley and drag me down until the sky disappeared forever.

It started out small.

I couldn't breathe through my nose. Then the infection spread to my mouth, my throat. I couldn't inhale, couldn't get enough air, like my body was rejecting oxygen, even though without it I would pass out.

"Mom," I called weakly. "Mom."

"Charlie?" she came back into the kitchen. "Are you all right? What's wrong? You look all red."

"Can't—can't—"

"Breathe, sweetie." Her hand felt nice on my back, her fingers five points of strength to concentrate on. "Did you eat too quickly? Food go down the wrong side?"

I shook my head. It was just like her to assume it was a physical problem, a logical problem. No one in the Dixon family would have a panic attack. That wouldn't make any sense, because every problem had a clear-cut answer; every problem could be talked through. Maybe in her world. I wished Granddad were here. He would see what it was all about, even if he didn't know the details.

"It's been a long week," I said, my voice hoarse. *I have to throw a game tomorrow. I have to decide what to do about the flash drive, the kids at school, Bridget, Ellie. If I could just pass out and skip everything tomorrow . . . if I could just pass out . . .*

"Why don't you come into the den, watch some TV. Get your mind off things?" she suggested. "We'll watch whatever you want." She smiled. "Even something with 'Extreme' in the title."

I wiped my eyes. "No, I'm okay, I'm okay. I have homework to do."

She tried to stroke my hair, but I dodged away. There was a

finality to the movements, like maybe this was the last time she and I would do that. I gathered my dishes and walked to the sink.

"Call us if you need anything," Mom said.

She just wanted someone to comfort. Was that so awful, really?

Maybe the real reason she liked Ryder was because he let her.

I logged on to instant messaging. Waited five minutes, cracked my knuckles. Paced around my room like an ultimate fighter waiting for his opponent to show up.

And there he was: BM.

"Hi, Badtz-Maru," I typed.

"You found it," BM typed back.

We chatted for a while.

It was very enlightening.

When we were done chatting, I sent a mass e-mail to BM, Maria Posey, Bridget, and Mr. Donovan.

"You're invited!" said the subject line jovially. It was a dick move, but I was in a dick mood. The body of the e-mail read: "To an auction. Winner takes all. I have the flash drive. It can be yours if the price is right. Saturday night, Quartz Hill. Map and address to follow."

THROWING THE GAME

ON FRIDAY, I PUT ALL THOUGHTS OF THE FLASH DRIVE ASIDE.
I had a game to lose.

I hadn't seen Ryder all day, but that wasn't uncommon. I sort of hoped he was hiding out at my house again, since that seemed the safest option.

Two-thirds of the school had turned out for the match, and about a hundred fans from Agua Dulce were bussed in as well, their faces painted white and green.

Our colors were red and yellow. The Palm Valley Desert Rats. I mean, Cats. I was the only rat. I felt sick during warm-ups, but I felt a little sick before most games, not just games where I was playing double agent. Were you still a double agent if the other side didn't know you were helping them?

Maybe something miraculous would happen, like a tied game for eighty minutes, and then an accidental own goal that bounced off my foot. Then Ryder would get his money, Griffin would lose his, no one at Palm Valley would hate me (for long), and I'd never have to actively work against my own team again.

I jogged past the stands and made sure to point the happy-go-lucky finger guns at the two clogged pores who'd helped me earlier in the week. I did this mostly to convince myself I still kept promises. They waved back, thrilled by the acknowledgment, their arms around their surprisingly existent girls, a bucket of popcorn shared between them.

My gaze drifted over the stands. My parents were here. Ellie was here.

Griffin was here.

And that's what did it, in the end. Injected me with the adrenaline and courage to focus and get this done. If Griffin had been a real older brother, a decent older brother, Ryder would be right here on the field with me. He would've risen to the top, the star player of the school. I was convinced of it. I wanted to see Griffin's rotten, crooked smirk disappear when he realized he was going to lose his money.

We took our positions and the ref blew the whistle and it was time. Floppy-haired, cokehead-looking Steve, my target, had a new attribute: besides the floppy hair, which you really shouldn't see in high school soccer, he was limping a little on his left side.

He saw me noticing and gave me a dirty look. I grinned back, full wattage. "Havin' a little trouble with your ACL?" I asked. "Gee, that suuuuucks."

"Shove it up your ass, Dixon," he retorted.

Ah, the thrill of competition brought out the most elegant use of language.

As usual, most of the action was at the opposite end of the field. Our team was good. I used to be part of that action. Now I kept track of it from afar.

Something miraculous happened pretty quickly, all right, but it wasn't in my favor. Agua Dulce surrendered a goal in the third minute. The third minute! It took me a second to remember I'd better look happy about it, so I raced over and jumped on Josh's back. He was startled and annoyed. We weren't buddies. During most games, we weren't even on the field at the same time. But he eventually indulged my high five.

Inside, I was burning with resentment: 1–0 meant I didn't just have to foul Steve and try to give him a penalty kick. Now I had to do it *twice*.

The crowd was chanting "De-lin-sky, De-lin-sky!"

Fuck Delinksy and his ability to pull the trigger from thirty yards out. That used to be me. I was feeling 347 different kinds of anger. The only one missing was "justified anger." Maybe Ellie was right about me; maybe I'd gotten more aggressive in the past year, and Coach wanted that aggression on defense. Or maybe—and it killed me to think this—maybe Delinsky was simply a better player than I was. Maybe I'd lost my touch, and defense was the only place Coach could transfer me and still keep me on the team.

If Ryder *had* been on the team, it occurred to me now, *he* would've been Delinsky, starting freshman year. Which meant maybe I never would've gotten to be a soccer star at all, however faded I was now. Maybe I wouldn't have had three years as a forward, and all the hype and visibility it entailed, and Ellie wouldn't have noticed me and sent me that note through the school newspaper. ("Which East Coast transplant doesn't want to be too Forward about her crush?") It didn't have to be *me*. Anyone who'd been forward that year might've ended up as Ellie's boyfriend. Maybe she and Ryder would've gotten together! Maybe it was better that Ryder...God, stop.

I shook my head as though I'd poured water on it and needed to shake off the drops from my hair and eyes. Josh looked at me like I was nuts. I went over to the sideline and grabbed a bottle and poured some real water on my face, just to have something to do. Not like I'd worked up a sweat in the three minutes since the game began. Fuck Delinsky. Fuck Griffin. Fuck me for having all these weird thoughts.

Finally, five minutes later, the action reached my area of the pitch. We gave the ball away at midfield, and one of the Agua Dulce players sent a pass to Steve. But he wasted no time in lofting it over to his teammate on the far side.

If Steve never personally took the ball to the net, I was dead. You can't foul what's not there. And I couldn't cover both sides at once; one half was Josh's area.

Speaking of Josh, he was determined to play his guy tight, and things got tangled up before the ball went over the endline and the ref called a corner kick for Agua Dulce. We lined up, and I elbowed Steve just to let him know he couldn't get away from me that easily. But Patrick blocked the header and controlled the ball and the Desert Cats were off on offense again for another few minutes.

The next time Steve got the ball, I acted fast, sliding feet-first and keeping my cleats up to trip him. Steve went down, but the ref let us play on. What the fracking hell?

I stole the ball and danced through traffic and the stands erupted for me. Well, gee, if they were going to be supportive . . . I chipped it ahead and to the left where Delinsky was waiting, and then prayed he didn't score again. It felt good to hear those cheers. It felt good to remind everyone I was still there, I still had the moves. And it also made it look like I was trying to win, which couldn't hurt.

Steve was still on the ground. I went over and held a hand out. He ignored me, stood on his own, and then leaned in to whisper a threat.

"You better cut that shit out," he said.

"Son," I said. "I'm just getting started."

Unfortunately, my words fell somewhat flat since the action was all taking place at the far end of the field. Delinsky tried another shot on goal, shaking off a tackle and firing from long range again. His touch was off, though, and his attempt hit the far post. The crowd strained forward in their seats, then let out a collective moan of disappointment when the ball bounced off. Another attempt was caught by Agua Dulce's goalkeeper.

I was already getting sick of Delinsky's grandstanding. This wasn't supposed to be a one-man show. If I'd still been the striker, you could bet I'd have shared the wealth, passed the ball to other guys instead of acting like I was the only one who could score.

Finally—finally—in the twenty-fifth minute Steve received a solid pass and zipped toward our goal. I waited till he got close to the penalty box and then I lunged and grabbed his arm, pulling and twisting him off the ball.

Whistles, chaos. I held my hands up, an innocent man even while assuming Steve would be awarded a penalty kick, make it, and tie the score. But then the ref jogged over, signaling offsides. Apparently the flag had been up all along. The perfect opportunity, and Steve was offsides!

I was back at zero.

The next time Steve got possession, I chose a different tactic. I made like I was running really hard after him—so hard that I tripped over my own feet. I hoped that would give him the space he needed to take a shot. But at the last second he passed off to a teammate, who tried to get too cute and had the ball stripped by Josh.

But when Josh tried to clear the ball, he shanked it, sending it sailing back across the field. Steve was closer to it than I was and he got possession. I went straight for his bad foot, the one he'd been limping on earlier. I "accidentally" nailed it with my cleats, really put the full force of my weight into it. He howled and went down.

I got a yellow card, which really should've been a red. But at least Steve got the penalty kick. At long friggin' last, I'd fulfilled my part of the plan.

And good on him—he converted. Even with his limp, or maybe in part because of it, he was a good faker. Made like he was aiming left and then sent the ball neatly in the right corner of the net, a topspin blast. Patrick was devastated. I couldn't bear to look at him.

At halftime, the score was still tied.

I headed to the locker room to cool off and drink my weight in water.

But the fountain was broken, and our assistant coach, Mr. Mitchell, hadn't brought the cooler in from outside yet. I headed down the hall to find a working fountain. When I turned the corner, my face connected with a fist.

I dropped like a bag of hammers.

THE BLUE-RASPBERRY
LOLLIPOP

WHEN YOU FIND YOURSELF TIED UP IN THE CHEM LAB SUPPLY
closet, surrounded by jars of formaldehyde, about to be maimed
by a microscope-wielding thug, it's a pretty good indication that
something in your life has gone wrong.

When the base of the microscope came down on my foot, I
blacked out.

When I woke up again, the room was fuzzy. Above me on the
shelves were all the items any self-respecting mad scientist could
want. Test tubes, filter paper, eye droppers, plastic funnels, red and
blue litmus test paper, safety goggles, glass stirring rods, Bunsen
burners, thermometers, custom rubber tubing, boxes of plastic
gloves, and scales.

"What's your problem?" said a voice. I blinked and refocused,
turning my head in the direction of the sound. "Why are you trying
to wreck my scholarship? If I'm injured no college will want me."

I could just make out a blurry shape above me.

Steve.

And pals. The pals were what worried me. The pals were the

size of buildings—no soccer players, they. These were wrestlers, football linebackers, or an unholy hybrid of the two.

Looking deranged and vengeful, Steve raised the microscope again, this time over my right foot, intending to wreck both my feet and make them even. Awfully considerate of him.

Before Steve could bring the microscope down, Ryder plowed into the supply closet out of nowhere and slammed Steve into the shelves, causing lab equipment to fall over.

"Don't! He's trying to help you, asshole. He's on our side. You friggin' moron." He slapped Steve across the face.

Steve's pals each grabbed one of Ryder's arms, but Steve waved them off.

"What are you talking about?" said Steve, looking cowed and patting his face lightly. "He's the one trying to maim me out there."

"He's trying to get you penalty kicks. He already got you one, didn't he? He's trying to help you win!"

"But—what—" Steve stopped and directed his next words to me. "So get called on a handball or something. Don't ram into me and stamp my bad foot!"

"A handball? What's the fun in that?" I wheezed.

"You nearly broke my ankle."

"You *did* break my foot, you psycho!" I sputtered from my place on the floor. "I'm going to kill you!"

Ryder untied me and I hobbled up to one foot. "I can't even play the second half now." I swayed from side to side, woozy with pain and adrenaline and fear and hatred. I came at Steve wildly, wishing

I could balance enough to head-butt him and knock his teeth out.

Ryder held me back, his hands firm on my shoulders, and looked me straight in the eyes. "I'm sorry, man," he said. "I'm so sorry. You'll still get your money, I swear—"

"I wasn't doing this for the money."

Ryder turned his attention back to Steve, his fury mounting. "I told you you'd win the game. Didn't I tell you? Why didn't you trust me?"

"You sicced your pit bull on me. How was I supposed to know that was part of the plan?" Steve whined.

"If you had your fuckin' eyes open, you woulda seen what was going on. Penalty kick after penalty kick. If you don't start paying attention, you don't deserve to be scouted."

My head felt shaky, and blackness threatened to overtake my vision again. I couldn't figure out what they were talking about. Wasn't the point of losing so that Ryder could break free of Griffin? So Griffin would be bankrupt and Ryder would have money to skip town? What did it possibly have to do with Steve being scouted?

"Let's get Charlie outside, get him some help." Ryder snapped his fingers at Steve's thugs, who jumped into action, sensing a new alpha to lead them.

Steve was nervous now. "Shit, man. I wish you'd told me."

"And I wish you weren't so fucking stupid."

This may be impossible to believe, but the weirdest thing, the most vivid thing about the situation—besides my incapacitating pain and dizziness—was Ryder's behavior. He didn't sound like himself. He was swearing a blue streak, smacking Steve around, issuing orders. Toward me, he was the same old Ryder—patient, cool, collected—kind, even. Toward Steve, he was acting like a boss. The Man in Charge.

He was acting like Griffin.

Steve and Ryder propped me up and carried me down the hall, one of my arms around each of their shoulders. I tried to walk, but even the slightest pressure on my foot was agony; enough to make me crumble. A microscope as a weapon. I'd never cared much for chemistry, but I didn't think it was capable of hating me back.

I could see the countdown clock at the edge of the field. Four minutes until the second half started. Coach saw us and sprinted over.

"Think fast," Ryder whispered in my ear. "We can turn Steve in, get an assault charge going, or say it was an accident. Whatever you want to do, I'll back you."

"But if I turn in Steve, they'll have to call the sheriff's department and cancel the game, and all this'll be for nothing."

"I don't care," said Ryder vehemently. "This never should've happened to you. What do you want to do?" And just like that, he was back to being Ryder, the kid who threw the bat for me. The kid I *knew*.

"Let's finish the game."

"What happened?" Coach bellowed.

"Nothing, just fooling around on the stairs, twisted my foot," I said. "I need an ice pack, I'll be fine."

Ryder and Steve set me down on the team bench and brought me Gatorade and ice packs.

Steve, looking pale and ill, went to rejoin his team, occasionally glancing back at me. I propped my foot up, and Coach asked me if I was all right.

Before I could answer, I pitched forward and threw up, and the next thing I knew, I was lying down in an ambulance, headed to the ER.

I was on a gurney, and Ellie sat beside me, clutching my hand, as we coasted through Palm Valley. She was sucking on a blue-raspberry lollipop, her favorite. "Charlie, your parents are right behind us. They're following in their car."

"I think I broke my foot. I can feel something shifting down there, in pieces . . ." I moaned.

"They said you were horsing around, that you fell down the stairs at halftime. What were you doing?"

"Um, maybe there really was water damage to the staircase last year."

"It's okay, don't talk." She smiled at me, but all I could see was Patrick's disappointed face during Steve's penalty kick, and the base of the microscope coming down on my foot.

"You were right. You said something bad was going to happen. You had that feeling, remember?" I gripped her hand tighter.

"I wish I'd been wrong. I wish I'd never said that." Her eyes shimmered wetly. "I just want you to be okay."

I closed my eyes and rested my head.

Ellie's fingers brushed against my temple, petting and caressing me. It felt so good, I could almost block out everything else.

"I want you to know something," she said softly. "I don't want to lose you next year. We'll figure something out."

It was almost worth it. The injury, the pain, the fear, to hear those words.

"I don't want to lose you, either," I said.

She kissed me, a sugary mess of blue-raspberry tongue. It tasted like summer, and fall.

"How'd you get the blue tongue?" the nurse asked. She looked familiar.

"My girlfriend. She likes blue-razz lollipops. They sell them at the games."

The nurse was familiar because I'd met her on Tuesday, when I'd peeked into Maria Salvador's room.

I was hooked up to an IV drip and my foot was elevated with an ice pack. The X-ray showed that my big toe was okay, but two of my smaller toes were fractured. My foot wasn't actually broken; only my toes got smashed. Steve's aim left something to be desired.

The doctor didn't think it was too serious. I was on a mild painkiller so the world felt soft and safe again, like it had never been any other way.

My tongue was blue. Ellie had kissed me. Ellie was my girlfriend again. She was coming to Lambert College with me.

My tongue was blue, because she'd kissed me.

My tongue was blue.

The kiss.

It left a residue.

Sugar, sugar.

"That's how Posey did it," I blurted out. And because of the painkillers, I had a goofy smile on my face, which I didn't intend to have. But you kind of had to admire Posey's sneakiness, no matter how terrible it was.

"That's how who did what?" the nurse said.

"That's how Maria Posey—*Sound of Music* Maria—dosed her. They were playing Spin the Bottle. Posey made sure her turn landed on Salvador, and she took a sugar cube of acid and tongue-kissed her, transferring the drug."

The Kiss. Sugar, Sugar. In Exile. It wasn't Chekhov titles. Or at least, it wasn't *just* Chekhov titles. Maria Salvador remembered what happened, or she remembered what happened just before a bunch of worse things happened. Her bizarre babblings when I'd seen her on Tuesday weren't incoherent. They were clues. An attempt to reach out.

"Go ahead, ask her. She'll tell you. She remembers. She just couldn't say it, you know? But she remembers. Ask Maria Salvador about the kiss, and the sugar cube, and Spin the Bottle. I know that's what happened, I know it."

The nurse looked disturbed and upset. "I would ask her, but she's in a coma. It happened last night."

While Mom and Dad were in the hospital cafeteria grabbing a bite, Granddad stuck around for a chat.

I motioned for him to sit closer, and I told him about the game, the whole truth; why I'd been fouling Steve, what he'd done to me in return.

To my surprise, he didn't mention Steve at all. "Your friend Ryder doesn't sound like a real friend," he said. "He sounds desperate. And desperate people are like pets you shouldn't have. They turn on you."

I frowned. The muscles in my face felt tight. "He's not a dangerous pet, Granddad. He's just a guy from a lousy family who got in over his head. If I hadn't helped him, I couldn't live with myself."

"And now look what you have to live with," he said, motioning to my foot.

"They said I'll be fine. I mean, not right away, but soon," I said. "I won't be able to play for a few weeks, that's all."

I upped the dosage on my IV because what else could I do? They'd taped my wrecked toes to the stable ones for support. It was called "buddy taping."

The phrase had made me laugh, in that sour way. I was taped to Ryder and he was taped to me, and if it caused me pain once in a while, that was the price of having a friend, right? He'd paid a price for having me as a friend a long time ago.

"I've been cut loose," Granddad added. "Pneumonia-free. I can go home now."

"Home home, or senior center home?" I asked.

"Senior center."

I was bummed.

"It's time. Time to sell the house. Time to move on," he said.

"Maybe I can take some days off school and we can fix the house up together, repaint it, refloor it, make it shine for the agent."

"Maybe," said Granddad, but what I heard was, "Probably not." I felt smaller under his gaze, like my hospital bed was receding and his chair was growing farther and farther away.

He was no longer proud of me.

Sometimes you can see the shift right when it happens, and seeing it does nothing to help you correct it. Awareness isn't power.

I hated the phrase "Those who cannot remember the past are doomed to repeat it." As if knowing something was going to happen made it in *any way* possible to avoid. No. If anything, knowing something beforehand made it even more inevitable. Like me in Little League, telling myself not to throw the bat but always doing it anyway. Or like Ellie moving here from New York but never intending to stay.

Except she was, wasn't she? She was staying here with me, even though I wasn't a soccer player anymore, even though I'd worked for Ryder. So why? What did she see in me, exactly? It wasn't my love of sci-fi and bad TV because she didn't know about that. It wasn't my kindness toward her brother; I'd used him.

The hospital cut me loose, too, with a page of instructions and nothing stronger than a bottle of Tylenol. At home, I watched a bit of TV in the den while keeping my foot propped up.

When Ellie came over, Mom told her I needed to rest, but Dad gave in and said we could have half an hour. Mom shot him a look that could burn through glass, but for some reason their contradictory responses didn't bother me anymore. They felt comforting, a much-needed dose of normalcy after a surreal day.

Ellie and I went up to my room, and the half hour played out like a soccer match, each minute important, vital.

Minutes one and two, I spent with my head resting on Ellie's thigh, making her confirm for me what she'd said in the ambulance. She didn't want to lose me.

Minutes three, four, and five, she filled me in on gossip from school; everyone was worried about me. And we'd lost the game. Apparently Josh's handball resulted in a penalty kick for Agua Dulce, putting them ahead.

"Huh," I said.

"What?" said Ellie.

"Nothing. Go on."

Minute six, we undressed to our underwear and got under the sheets and started kissing. I couldn't get enough of her hair, which fell on my chest like a curtain I could lift again and again to start the show.

She settled on me like a soft, satin pillow, careful not to jar my foot. My skin was cool where the sheets touched me, and warm where Ellie curled against me. It was the perfect combination of opposites, like ice cream on a scorching summer day; or hot chocolate on a cold winter one; or the moment, in the blaze of the unforgiving, endless desert, when you reach the oasis—and for the first and only time, the mirage is real. The water is yours and it will never run out.

Minute seven, Ellie said, "I couldn't stand seeing you in pain, thinking you might not be able to play soccer again. I wanted another chance, to get things right, to get *us* right. I kept thinking about what you said in my room yesterday."

"Can you be more specific?"

She shimmied up my body and gave me a playful swipe on the nose. "Well, I didn't record and transcribe our conversation—"

"Why not?"

"—but I do remember we talked about you holding back. I think if we don't hold back, if we're honest from now on, we'll be fine."

I removed a condom from my bedside dresser.

I stroked Ellie's face and collected her tears with my thumbs, gently smearing them away and kissing them for good measure, absorbing them into my lips, my own body.

"Okay," I said, gently unclasping her bra. "This is me, not holding back."

Minutes eight through thirty were too blissful for broadcast.

THE AUCTION

ON SATURDAY, I SLEPT LIKE A LOG STUFFED WITH SLEEPING pills until I heard a knock on my bedroom door around noon. Having discarded my virginity like a heap of clothes on the floor, and having discarded my clothes on the floor like a heap of virginity, I scrambled to get dressed, and barely noticed the throbbing in my toes.

"Uh, come in," I said.

Dad, looking for all the world like he'd brokered the happiness I was currently experiencing—and maybe he had, by letting Ellie stay for a while last night—said, "Lunch is ready, and Ryder's eating it, so you might want to skedaddle. Need any help getting downstairs?"

"I'm good," I said. "Thanks. See you in five."

I grabbed my cell phone off my desk and felt my chest expand with warmth at the sight of a text from Ellie.

It was time-stamped two hours ago: "Money's on the dresser, doll."

I grinned and texted back: "First taste is free."

Ellie, two seconds later: "Damn. I'm already hooked."

Me: "That's how we get you."

She'd clearly been keeping her phone close, waiting for me to text back; her responses were that immediate. It was strange, knowing I had the advantage now, probably for the first time since we'd started dating. I considered making her wait and second-guess herself. I could go downstairs for lunch, hang out with Ryder, and text her at random intervals throughout the day, just to show her how it felt to be at the emotional mercy of someone else.

Instead, I decided to call her. Why play games?

I'd be lying if I said the urge wasn't there, though. Just for a second. The urge to punish her.

"I'm your doll, huh?" I said when she picked up.

"I think I get why people smoke cigarettes now. I almost stopped for some on the way home," she said.

"As long as they weren't cloves," I said. "You'd have to join the drama kids."

"You know what I remember most? Besides the obvious?" she asked, her voice low and secretive and pleased.

"What's that?" I asked, smiling, happy I'd manned up and called her. My groin was kind of happy, too. Her voice seemed different to me now, because I'd heard it having sex. I knew what it was capable of doing. Why would I want to miss out on the morning-after banter? We only had one chance to get it right.

"The way you draped your arm across my body afterward."

I pictured us the night before, spent, Ellie on her back and me on my stomach beside her, our eyes closed, my arm curled over her slender waist as we surged and reached for breath.

"Yeah? Why's that?"

"It was like the safety bar on a roller coaster. Holding me in, but not too tight, just enough to keep me safe."

"We operate twenty-four hours a day. No lines," I said.

"Do you have plans tonight?"

"Yeah, I'm going to get to the bottom of the flash drive situation. Kinda boring, but I want to be done with it." I didn't give her the details because I figured she'd disapprove and I didn't want to find out if I was right.

"Speaking of the flash drive, I meant to tell you something about Mr. Donovan."

"Yeah, hot, talk Donovan to me," I teased. "How do you mean?"

"He's a Ziploc washer. I saw him one time in the chem lab when I had to stay late, and he didn't know right away I was there. It was miserably awkward."

Mom used to make me do the same thing with my bagged lunches in grade school. It embarrassed me, saving them and carefully turning them inside out to brush off the crumbs over the trash can while the other kids cavalierly tossed theirs away. Only people on tight budgets (or people like my mom, who remembered what it was like to be on tight budgets) would think to do such a thing. Donovan and my mom were part of the same tribe.

Ellie's memory jogged one of my own. I'd seen Donovan at the Goodwill store last summer when I'd dropped off a bag of clothes. He'd been browsing, finding a cheap pair of corduroys and a buttondown. His tweed jacket with the elbow patches didn't seem like an affectation anymore. It seemed like the best he could find.

"He's not changing the grades for monetary gain," Ellie finished. "If he's making a bonus, he's not keeping it. So. I think I was wrong about him."

"Good to know," I said. But it didn't actually make a difference to me, and I knew it wouldn't make a difference to BM, either.

Someone was going to pay tonight at the auction, and pay big.

Ellie and I reluctantly hung up after realizing we wouldn't be seeing each other until Monday. She was taking Jonathan to Maxwell Park and Wildwater Kingdom tomorrow as a reward from their parents for being eligible to skip a grade.

I hobbled down to the kitchen and saw that Ryder wasn't the only person at the table. He was sitting next to Deputy Thompson, and they were . . . getting along. It was weird. Granddad was there, too, looking friendlier than he had last night.

"I told them about Steve," said Ryder, glancing at Thompson. "We can go after him for what he did to your foot, but it might be tricky because it's basically your word against his, or we can go after him for drug trafficking, which carries a minimum sentence of three years." Ryder practically bounced in his seat. "Right?"

"Right," said Deputy Thompson, digging into his turkey sandwich. Whatever qualms he'd once had about breaking bread in our household were long gone.

"Drug trafficking?" I sputtered. Cokehead-looking Steve was a cokehead! A book and its cover were never better matched.

"Yeah, he's Griffin's distribution for Agua Dulce. Steve's got a whole team of dealers fanning out from there to Van Nuys. Tonight's the buy, under the 14 Freeway. It's a desperation sale, so Griffin can recoup some of his losses from the game. If the LSD's still bad, or has strychnine or something in it, we can't let it hit the streets."

If I'd had any doubts about Ryder's loyalty, I didn't anymore. Griffin was the dangerous animal, not Ryder. Ryder was trying to put a stop to it all. He looked positively giddy at the thought of sending his brother away. I couldn't exactly blame him, but then, I'd never had a sibling try to force-feed me bad LSD. Being an only child had its perks.

I thought about Ryder and Griffin's mom then, and whether she knew about the Shakespearean-level betrayal about to go down under her own roof. Whether she would wonder about her own part in the story. Then I got to wondering whether Ryder blamed her as much as he blamed Griffin; she was supposed to protect him.

I wanted to join them on the bust, but it wasn't happening till after sundown, and I had another engagement. Also, Deputy Thompson didn't want to take any unnecessary risks; he needed Ryder along to point out the exact location of the meet, and to ID his brother, but I would get in the way. Besides, Mom and Dad wanted me to rest.

I did convince them to let me go to a "study group" in Quartz Hill a few hours later. After all, I only needed my right foot to drive.

We sat in folding chairs, in a circle in Granddad's vacant living room, like we were playing Russian roulette. I couldn't figure out which one of us was the triggerman, and then I realized that meant it was me. I didn't exactly cut an imposing figure, what with my black eye and my foot in a special shoe that made me lopsided, but maybe the combination made me seem either dangerous or crazy, and both worked to my advantage. The only man you don't mess with is the man who's got nothing to lose, because what he's got, he doesn't value. I had something they all wanted, but the dirty tests meant nothing to me, so I could negotiate all night and into next week if I had to.

Everyone was glancing nervously at me and then glancing away just as nervously, like they weren't sure if making eye contact would help or hurt their respective causes.

Mr. Donovan sat to my left, fidgety and anxious; Bridget sat to my right, huffy and puffy. Maria Posey sat directly across from me, looking like she was about to go clubbing afterward, or possibly like she already had gone clubbing and the evening had been a disappointment because the band member she'd messed around with the week before hadn't dedicated a song to her.

We couldn't start till BM arrived, though. I'd decided to give him the opening bid.

"Indulge my curiosity for a minute," I said, twirling a pencil in my hand.

"We're here for one reason, and it's not to indulge your curiosity, *Charlie*," snapped Maria Posey. Ever since I learned about Maria

Salvador's coma yesterday, I couldn't refer to either girl by their cutesy nicknames anymore. Calling Maria Salvador anything other than her real name diminished her and diminished what had happened to her, so from now on they were Posey and Salvador, the way they always should've been.

"Well, I don't happen to like the way you say my name, *Miz Posey*, so until you tell me what I want to know, nobody gets the flash drive. Got it? Start at the beginning. Tell me what happened to make you all go after this poor girl. Did you really want her out of the way just so you could get a damn concert solo?"

"The solo?" Posey sputtered. "The solo had nothing to do with it. It was always about the tests."

Bridget snorted, and Posey sent her a death glare.

"It was a pleasant side effect, though, wasn't it?" I said. "How'd you find out about the tests?"

Posey sighed and flipped her hair. "She *told* me. She thought I'd be angry and, like, storm the next school board meeting with her, demanding Donovan's resignation."

If Mr. Donovan was miffed at the lack of "Mister" ahead of his name, he gave no indication of it. He gave no indication of anything, least of all that he was here, now, in the room with us. No, he was someplace else entirely. The room he was in probably had soft classical music playing and an iced-tea dispenser in the corner, and no chance of pitting him against his students for the right to own a cover-up.

Posey had no right to share a name with the person she'd

damaged. Posey must have noticed her identity had shifted in my head, because she sought to recapture my attention. Head songbirds didn't like being dismissed. She wanted center stage even in this absurd venue.

"I'd just gotten my early acceptance letter from Barnard! It was like, are you kidding me? You want me to call the admissions office and confess? To something I didn't even do?"

"I get it," I said, my words dripping with poisoned honey. "You had no choice but to put her in a coma. No other options whatsoever."

"Hey, *West Side Story* Maria agreed; when I told her how many lives it would wreck, she came around and said yes to the payoff. She didn't feel right screwing other people over when it wasn't their fault, when no one else knew about Donovan. It was a bullshit move, changing her mind like that at the last second."

"I get it," I said again. "She couldn't be bought, so she had to be silenced. You drugged her."

Posey wheeled on her former consigliere. "It was Bridget's idea!"

"*I said, 'Get her drunk,'* " Bridget screeched. "I didn't want her *silenced.*"

Posey stood up. "It *wasn't* my fault."

"You kissed her," I said. "You shoved your sugary tongue into her mouth and forced her to go on the drug trip from hell."

Mr. Donovan blinked a few times and opened his mouth to speak but then didn't say anything. He may have peeked through the door from his room to ours, but he wasn't ready to walk inside.

"I didn't mean for that to happen," Posey insisted. "That wasn't supposed to happen. Ryder said—"

"Ryder said what?"

"That it goes away the second you fall asleep. He said being on LSD is like dreaming while you're awake, so once you *do* go to sleep, and start dreaming for real, it knocks the drug right out of you."

"Or maybe it makes it so you *can't* sleep," I snapped. "Ever think of that?"

"But then Ryder wouldn't give me any LSD anyway, so—"

"You're the one who called Griffin," I said, suddenly realizing it.

"He knows how much the flash drive's worth. He wanted to help, didn't even charge me for the tab."

"Because he didn't know if the LSD was any good. Are you following along here? Do you get how serious this is yet? He gave you a free tab because he needed to know if it was any good."

"Well, *I* was fine. I tripped for a few hours and lay me down to sleep," Posey insisted. "It wasn't a bad batch."

"Have you even visited Salvador in the hospital? Because when I saw her, she hadn't slept in forty-eight hours. If she wasn't crazy before, she is now."

"Why are you yelling at me? For the last time, it was *her* idea!" Posey turned and pointed a long, bony, shaking finger at Bridget.

"I said 'Get her drunk and take embarrassing photos.' I *didn't* say give her LSD!"

"Embarrassing photos?" I asked.

"For leverage. Thought we could dummy up a Facebook page

and send the link to her college of choice so they'd reject her for underage partying. Something to force her to hand over the flash drive."

I gaped at Bridget. "Is blackmail your default answer to *everything?*"

"I said 'Get her drunk,'" Bridget repeated, on a loop.

I wanted to tell her to refresh her homepage.

"I tried, it was impossible, she's like a monk," Posey retorted.

Mr. Donovan finally spoke. His voice was tired and his words circled the girls' throats like lassoes, squeezing them into silence. "You stupid children. She's already on lithium. You could've killed her."

Don't count them out yet, I thought. They still might.

"So it wasn't a bad batch," I said. "It was only a bad batch for Maria Salvador."

"I didn't know," Posey wailed. "It's not my fault."

"How did *you* know about the lithium?" I asked Mr. Donovan.

"They give the teachers relevant health information at the beginning of the year in case something ever happens in class."

Ellie'd told me Maria was the last person on earth who'd take drugs or alcohol. Because she'd known any interactions could be harmful, even fatal.

I turned back to Bridget. "What made you so sure the flash drive was in the library?"

"Just a guess."

My eyes strongly suggested she guess harder.

"Fine, like I told you before, I saw *West Side Story* Maria—"

"Stop calling her that. Call her by her real name."

Bridget cleared her throat. "I saw Maria Salvador on Friday at the library second period. When the bell rang, she was conferring with a librarian, looking shifty, and then they disappeared into a back room."

"To get the Chekhov key," I said.

"I didn't think much about it until the party, when I heard her tell *this genius* she'd hidden it at school," Bridget added. "I needed to know who else was there second period and might've seen her hide it, or might've taken it for themselves."

"You just needed the right patsy to interview the people you didn't have access to," I muttered.

"I also needed to work fast. While you were *slowly* making your way through the front of the list, I tackled the back of it."

"What were you going to do?" Posey said to Bridget, deadpan. "If you'd found the flash drive?"

"Sell it to you," I answered for Bridget. "For three times the price. Make you think it was Ellie brokering the deal so you wouldn't send Griffin after her."

"She didn't think it was fair," said a male voice.

A Hispanic man of about twenty had let himself in. He sat down in the last available seat. Everyone shifted to face him.

"Badtz-Maru?" I said.

He nodded without looking at me. But really I'd come to think of him as Brother de Maria.

"He's here. Can we start now?" Posey said.

"She couldn't live with herself," BM continued, in a manner that told us he was settling in for a story and anyone who didn't like it was free to leave empty-handed. "She needed the money, but she couldn't live with herself. That's why she changed her mind. She was writing a college essay, and it hit her that every word would be a lie if she pretended her grades were true. And if every word was a lie, why was she going to college at all? What was she hoping to get out of it that would feel worth doing, if getting there took what it took? And she started to think about the person she'd be displacing at the university, the person whose spot she stole through tampered grades. And then she started to wonder if Mr. Donovan was the only teacher at Palm Valley padding the scores, or if it was endemic across every subject in every grade. She became obsessed. She and the newspaper editor, Jane Thomas, decided to find out. They were working together to prove other teachers were involved. *If* other teachers were involved. But she never got the chance."

I remembered Thomas' English Muffin closing her computer window when I'd walked into the journalism room.

Mom, I thought, with increasing alarm. What did you do? By making Fresh Start's tests the only way to measure knowledge and progress, what did you do? It wasn't her fault. But a remarkably high number of people were not to blame, and getting higher. "And the thing is," BM said, his voice rising, "her grades were *good*."

He turned his chair so he was looking at Mr. Donovan, who reluctantly looked back.

"No, they weren't perfect," BM admitted, "but she would've *worked* for it. You didn't need to change her scores. You needed to teach her better."

"Well, my debate team isn't so lucky," said Mr. Donovan, a fire in his voice. "If I didn't meet the test quota, they would've lost their funding. What about them? What about *their* college prospects? I wanted to make a difference for them. Memorizing random dates and facts until you've regurgitated them onto a multiple-choice test and not a second longer wasn't helping them become better scholars! Debate *means* something to them. Forming arguments, seeing both sides of an issue, learning to think critically, facing their fears of public speaking—they *lived* for that one Saturday a month they could shine. They needed something in their lives to be proud of. I couldn't take that away from them."

I thought of their third-place trophy in the cabinet in Mr. Donovan's classroom, how he kept it polished and gleaming.

"I know it was wrong. I didn't think I had a choice. My contract's up for renewal every single year. Every bonus I made went straight into to the team fund: bus rentals, travel expenses, photocopies, books, food for after-school practice . . ."

"You have a choice now," I said. "How many zeroes are you willing to add to the number five?"

"You're a cold son of a bitch," BM snarled.

"Wait'll you find out who the bitch in question is," Bridget said. "Fresh starts for all?"

I ignored her. If I acknowledged her words in any way, I would lose it. "Opening bid is five hundred dollars. Who's got it?"

"It's kind of sick how much you're enjoying this," Bridget said.

"Says the girl who planned on doing the exact same thing."

"I don't have much money," said BM.

"You don't have five hundred dollars? What about your car? Mine's called Amelia, and she's been having some trouble lately. I could use an upgrade."

"Five hundred fifty," said Mr. Donovan, looking ill.

"Six hundred," said Bridget.

"She's just going to turn around and blackmail the rest of us," Posey protested. "It'll never end! She shouldn't be allowed to bid."

"Easy fix. Outbid her," I enunciated.

"Five thousand," Posey shot back.

"Now we're getting somewhere," I said, and laughed.

"My car's worth six," BM blurted out. "You can have my car."

Mr. Donovan swallowed. "This is madness. If I'm losing my job anyway, I can't be spending this kind of money."

"Then I guess you better hope Posey wins, since you both want the same thing," I said. "Pool your resources."

"I can contribute two hundred more," he said weakly.

"Six thousand seven hundred fifty," Posey told me promptly.

"What do you need the money for?" Bridget asked me. "You're getting seventy percent off tuition as it is."

"Maybe I want to take Ellie to prom."

"Where? Vegas?"

My phone beeped. "Oh, good! It's the pizza," I said. "Just kidding. It's an off-site bidder. Just kidding—"

Posey leapt toward me and grabbed my shirt collar in her bony fist. "Quit screwing around. Make a decision."

I peeled off her fingers and shoved them at her, turning away to hunch over my phone and read the text message that had just come in. It was from Ryder: "Nailed 'em."

One down, one to go. I was feeling mighty pleased with myself.

"Now, where was I? Oh, yes. Six thousand seven hundred fifty … going once, going twice—"

"My car, plus oil changes, tire rotations, and maintenance for a year, on the house," BM cried out. "I work part-time at a gas station."

"Tempting. At seventy-five bucks a pop, once a month, that's about … Hmm, I was never good at multiplication. Too bad you weren't my math teacher," I said to Mr. Donovan. "Then it wouldn't matter."

"Seven grand, final offer," said Posey.

BM jumped up and hurled his folding chair against the wall. "I don't have anything else to give you." He got in Posey's face. "You ruined her life. Live with that, *puta*. All of you."

The folding chair still had some fight left in it, so for good measure, BM kicked it over and left the room.

"Where's my flash drive?" said Posey.

"Where's my money?" I said.

"In two installments once I turn eighteen next month."

"No. First installment now, and make it five grand since you obviously have access to that much, and I give you a copy of the flash drive. Second installment arrives, I give you the original."

"Fine. Right now?"

"Right now."

She pulled a variation of the Velvet Rope pose from her party, one hand on her hip, other hand extended and open, as if still waiting for me to produce my invite.

"It's not *on* me," I snapped. "You think I've been carrying it around? Did you see what Maria's brother did to that chair? Meet me in the park in twenty minutes. Can you get the cash by then?"

In response she produced a check from her purse. The original five grand intended to buy off Salvador.

"It's already made out to Charlie *Dix*on. How'd I say your name this time?" she retorted.

Everybody went their separate ways.

As we'd planned, BM was waiting for me in the backseat of my car, crouched low.

"Seven thousand," he marveled. "I didn't think she'd take the bait."

"Sorry to be such a jerk in there. I had to get the numbers up, had to make you sound desperate," I said.

He scratched his nails through his hair. "I couldn't think of anything else to sell. I should've gone higher."

"No, any higher and she would've gotten suspicious. I liked your shtick about working at a gas station, though."

BM smirked. "I am but a humble pobrecito Mehican. People like her can't imagine me in pre-med."

"It was inspired. And you got more than what she was going to pay your sister," I reminded him.

He looked conflicted. "I wanted to let Maria decide what to do with the drive. I hate letting that spoiled princess get away with hurting her. But the most important thing is putting a dent in the hospital bills and hiring a private nurse for a while. Thanks, man. I owe you one."

We shook hands. "I'll get the check from Posey tonight and sign it over to your bank Monday morning."

By the time I reached Ellie's, it was 10:30, a wee bit late to come a-calling, but it didn't seem to bother her.

"I didn't think I'd get to see you tonight," she said, standing on her tiptoes and greeting me with a kiss.

"Surprise," I said, kissing her back. "I can't stay."

"Who's there?" called her father.

"I think my parents would agree," said Ellie.

Ellie's dad appeared, mug of tea in hand. "Are you okay, Charlie?" he said. Translation: Why are you here, and when are you leaving?

"I'm fine, sir." I looked pointedly at Ellie for the next part. "I just remembered I left a flash drive here, and I need it for a test."

Drift received, Ellie glided upstairs to get it.

"Sorry to stop by so late. I know you're off to Maxwell Park tomorrow, so I thought I'd better grab it tonight," I explained to Ellie's father.

Sometimes I'm so good with adults it's eerie.

Ellie returned, looking pale.

"What's wrong?" I said, reaching her side at once, gently searching her expression.

"It's—it's not there."

"I left it in your room, on your desk," I said slowly and carefully, feeling something shake loose inside me and drop into the pit of my stomach, where it rolled around like a marble.

"I know. I can picture exactly where it was, but it's not there anymore."

We heard a door opening and closing above us, and I looked up, where Jonathan stood at the top of the stairs, in his pajamas and glasses. His hand was curled around something.

"I have the flash drive," he said, standing perfectly still.

"What are you doing awake?" Ellie's dad asked him. "Time for bed, you've got a big day tomorrow."

"J-Dawg, why do you have the flash drive?" Ellie said in barely tethered exasperation.

"It doesn't belong to you," I added. "Can I have it back?"

"It's not yours, either," he said.

"Jonathan, give it back to Charlie," ordered Ellie's dad.

Jonathan remained at the top of the stairs, his body a fixed line, his face a mixture of defiance and fear.

I strode up the steps. "May I take a look at it?"

Jonathan glanced from his father to his sister before shoving the drive into my hand; his palm was sweaty. The penguin sticker was still intact and the drive didn't seem to be damaged, but I had to make sure. I moved immediately into Ellie's bedroom and approached her desk.

Ellie was two seconds behind me.

"What's all this stuff?" I asked, looking at a series of colorful pamphlets spread across every surface. They were brochures for colleges; colleges that weren't Lambert. Included in the stack of papers was an acceptance letter from MECA—Maine College of Art. "We are pleased to offer you a spot in the class of 2018 . . ."

"Let me clear those away," she said quickly, sliding the brochures off the edge of her desk and into the trash below. "It's just for my dad, so he thinks I've covered all the bases."

She didn't sound sincere—she sounded like she'd been caught. I couldn't process that information because I had to finish what I'd started with BM before I could handle any other problems in my life. I inserted the flash drive into her laptop.

It was blank.

No dated folders to click on, nothing.

The entire drive had been wiped clean.

"He . . . he erased it," I said, feeling my legs bend like broken stilts. There was nothing to do but slide to the floor.

Jonathan's eyes filled with water and spilled over. "I heard you the other day. I heard you talking. You said Mr. Donovan would get fired. But if he gets fired, there won't be any debate team, and then I won't have a group and no one will protect me. I don't want to end up like Ryder." Fat tears rolled down his cheek, gathering speed as he closed his eyes against the pain. "I needed to know there was a place for me, a place I would belong."

THE OTHER TRUTH
ABOUT RYDER

MONDAY AFTERNOON, I SAT IN HISTORY CLASS, MY USUAL seat, right by the window. It had only been a week since Bridget hired me to find the flash drive, but I felt years older.

The morning's *Palm Valley Register* included a splashy article about Griffin's arrest. He'd been caught red-handed by Deputy Thompson, trying to offload cocaine and LSD under the 14 Freeway Saturday evening. He remained in the sheriff's custody, as did Steve from Agua Dulce—though on lesser charges, since Steve hadn't actually reached for his wallet at the time of the bust.

Mr. Donovan and I pretended we'd never spoken two words to each other. When I reached under my desk on the off chance there might be an envelope full of trouble there, the way there had been last Monday, I discovered two hundred-dollar bills and a Post-it note taped to the bottom instead. I carefully unpeeled them. "For Maria Salvador," the Post-it read. "More when I can get it."

I almost laughed. Two hundred dollars would cover about fifteen minutes of her hospital stay. I had the urge to stand up in front of him and the whole class and tear the bills in half. Two hundred wasn't worth a damn, not when we'd almost had seven thousand. Almost this, almost that. Almost was worse than nothing. I didn't know how I could possibly face BM after e-mailing him the bad news yesterday.

Ellie was suffering through chemistry in the classroom right behind mine. She and I had plans to hang out after school, since I obviously wouldn't be going to soccer practice, and I wanted to be thrilled about it—I knew I should be thrilled about it—but I was still fixating on the MECA acceptance letter she'd swept off her desk the other night.

The past week had taken a toll on me, and the toll got more expensive as the hour wore on. When the bell rang, I hobbled toward the door, the last to leave. Or so I thought. I'd forgotten one of my notebooks, so I doubled back and saw something peculiar: Josh, unlocking the window, exactly the way I used to.

Ellie and I went out for coffee. Ironically, we chose Café Kismet. All the holiday decorations were gone and it seemed different from last time. Even so, I made sure we didn't sit at the same table as before. She apologized a thousand times about Jonathan. I let her, and I bought her a peppermint drink and we split a chocolate croissant.

People saw us; waved and smiled. It was nice. It was better than nice. I existed again, I was solid and sober, and Ellie was my girlfriend. For the whole afternoon, I let myself believe in the fantasy. I sank right down into it like a soft downy bed and the promise of ten-hour sleep. I let myself believe next year would be more of the same, being sweet and easy and good with each other.

After coffee we went to the mall for more hand-holding, and we kissed for a long time in my car before she walked into her house. After dinner I told my parents there was a soccer meeting to discuss strategy for the next few games, and when it got dark, I headed back to school. They thought I was a team player. *Even injured, he's one of the gang.*

Could I really fault Jonathan for erasing the drive, if he thought there were only two options available to him: join debate or turn into Ryder?

It was time to see what it was Ryder had turned into.

I waited outside the history classroom in the dark. I watched as Ryder strolled over and swung up onto the window ledge and heaved open the window to crawl inside.

And then I followed him.

But he wasn't there.

He had vanished.

There was a sliver of light emanating from the supply closet, so I hobbled toward it and opened the door. Inside, one of the cheap portable shelves had been rolled aside to reveal a second door, which led into the chemistry lab closet; the classrooms were tied together like adjacent hotel suites. On one of the rearranged shelves, hidden behind a stack of books, was a metal container, which had recently been opened. I looked inside; it was empty.

It made sense now. How Ryder had found me in the chem lab closet during Friday's game, with Steve and his thugs. At the time, it felt like Ryder had appeared out of nowhere, which I chalked up to my blackouts and pain, but he'd really found us by walking through the history classroom, which was open for the debate team's use. He'd entered the lab through the supply closet—and had been doing so for months. With my help. Unlocking the history window had nothing to do with Mr. Donovan, or history class. It was always about the chemistry lab. If I'd been taking chemistry last period, he could've skipped a step and gone through *that* window instead.

Ryder faced away from me, iPod buds in his ears, hunched over one of the black lab tables, intent on his work.

"Hey!" I yelled.

He whirled around and pulled his earbuds out, nearly tripping over his backpack. "Jesus, you scared me. What are you doing here?"

On the desk were trays and blotting paper, a bag of sugar cubes, and a couple of droppers. Spread out in front of him, in a straight line, were about twenty orange Tic Tacs. He had lined up the sugar cubes beside them. Each Tic Tac represented an order to fill. I figured it was a way to help him count, make sure he had the correct number of hits each week as the orders fluctuated.

Ryder was using the chem lab as a place to store, measure, and bag LSD. He'd never be found with drugs on him or at his mother's trailer because he hid them right at school, in a locked metal container under a mound of unused textbooks. And then he came here at night to assemble them into tabs or sugar cubes.

"Griffin's done, man," he crowed. "We did it."

Ryder pulled me in for a hug, but I stepped away.

"If Griffin's done, why are you here? Why are you doing this?"

He shrugged. "Griffin's drugs were ass. Mine are pure Orange Sunshine. I've never pushed them on anyone, and I only sell to people who know what they're getting into. What happened with Salvador . . . I tried to stop them."

I was horrified. "I've been helping you. I've been leaving the window unlocked. I've been helping you and I didn't even know it."

Ryder rolled his eyes. "It had nothing to do with you."

"There's a girl in a coma because of us! Don't you care?"

"I didn't sell to her. I would *never* dose someone against her will," he said forcefully.

"The amount of things you'd 'never do' could fill a fucking Tweet."

"Trust me, getting rid of Griffin just made this town a whole lot safer."

"Why, because of the strychnine? I looked that up. Nobody laces LSD with strychnine; it's an urban legend cops and teachers tell kids to scare them. Deputy Thompson probably even believes it. I did, too."

"Look who has a Wiki app on his phone," Ryder said sarcastically.

"You didn't want Griffin in jail so he'd *stop*," I realized. "You wanted Griffin in jail so you could take over."

I clenched my key chain in my fist, about to crush it. I knew it'd leave an imprint in my palm.

Ryder half smiled. He looked almost pleased I'd figured it out; that he would get credit from someone for having masterminded the coup. "I cut out the middle man, too," he said. "Nailing Steve was a bonus. Now I control all the guys who worked for him."

"No more Steve, no more Griffin," I reiterated slowly. "It's all you now. Why did you have me throw the game? I bet there wasn't even any money at stake."

"There was a shit-ton of money at stake. Steve was done with dealing, he wanted out by the summer. It meant nothing to him. It was a lark, it was ski-trip money; he didn't *need* the money—not the way I needed it. He wanted to play soccer for some school in the Midwest, wanted a good showing at the game on Friday. I told him I'd guarantee him the win if he handed over his list of buyers and dealers to me after graduation. I figured I'd take over after he left for college."

"But then you got impatient, didn't want to wait that long."

"I was pissed at him for busting up your foot."

"Yeah, right. You don't give a crap about that. You wanted Griffin and Steve out of the way, and now they are."

"I tried to protect you," he said, putting a hand on my shoulder. "You weren't supposed to get hurt."

"You were just protecting yourself. You used me because you knew I still feel like I owe you."

Ryder's face transformed into a mask of rage. "You *do* owe me."

"Little League was six years ago!" I cried.

His mask cracked, revealing genuine confusion. "Little League?

Who the fuck said anything about Little League? What are you talking about?"

"When you threw the bat for me, got me into soccer, made sure I had friends going into seventh grade."

He looked really uncomfortable. "You think I did that for you? I was bored with baseball and I hated Coach Tierson. I just wanted to mess with him."

"You did it to help me. You threw away a real shot at baseball to help me."

Ryder shook his head, refused to look me in the eyes. "Nobody has a friend like that," he said. "Nobody has a friend that good."

But *I* had. I know I had. It was Ryder who didn't have a friend like that.

Not a single friend good enough to risk his own neck to help him freshman year. I'd abandoned him. I'd stuck to the soccer team; I'd let him drown, let him get picked off by the bullies and the druggies, with only his brother to save him. Which was worse than not being saved at all.

"Then why did you think I owed you?" I asked.

"My mom's painkillers are what started this. After we had to move, after she got beat up on the job and my dad went to prison defending her, she got hooked on pills and Griffin started skimming off the top and selling them. It wasn't long before he graduated into harder stuff."

"You said you never blamed me for your family's shit."

"I didn't. I don't. I'm just telling you cause and effect. Do we have a problem?" he said, indicating the miniature assembly line behind him.

"No."

"Are you going to tell anyone about this?"

"How can I, without implicating myself?" I pointed out.

"You can't. You're part of it. Every payoff proves it."

Maybe he had bought my silence, but not with money. He'd bought it on the baseball field six years ago, and the price was high, higher than I could've imagined. And now we didn't even have that.

"I warned you," Ryder said. "I told you to let it go. I did warn you."

"Why?"

He shrugged. "Old habit. Like smoking."

If Ryder and I hadn't become friends, what would my life in Palm Valley have been like? Would I have been a pariah going into seventh grade, as I'd always feared, or would people have forgotten about the events of the summer? Could I have owned up to my sci-fi leanings, or would that have been social suicide?

Who was I at Palm Valley High if not a beckham?

"It was Josh who framed me," I said quietly. "He's the one who drove Salvador to the hospital in my car."

"He wanted you out of Friday's game. He figured you'd be so distracted by the sheriff's department, or drinking so much, that Coach would have to bench you."

"And now he's the one unlocking the window for you."

"He proved himself by throwing the game after you got sent out," Ryder said matter-of-factly.

"Oh, well, good for him. He's a better version of me than I am."

Josh hadn't wanted me out of the game so he could play; he'd wanted me out of the game so he could cheat. He'd been on Ryder's payroll all along, same as me.

"He didn't trust you to get the job done. He didn't think you'd screw over Patrick and the rest of the guys like that. To be honest, neither did I," Ryder said.

I felt like throwing up, so I turned around to leave the way I'd come in. "You take care, now. Don't forget to lock up when you're done," I muttered.

"Charlie, come on."

I whirled around, giving in to my fury for a split-second. "What?"

"I think you were grateful the rest of that summer, maybe even the rest of junior high. But I think part of you was furious that I had to step in and save you. That you were too much of a pussy to stand up to Coach yourself."

"Sure, why not," I said, pushing down every ounce of emotion I possessed. I wouldn't freak out in front of him. I wouldn't point out that the last person to call me a pussy had been Coach Tierson himself. "If it makes you feel better."

"And you were more than happy to take my money these last few months. Don't act you like didn't benefit."

"I'm not acting. This is me, not acting. This is me, walking away. Can I walk away now? With my one good foot?"

I calmly hobbled through the chem lab closet door and back into the history classroom.

My veins filled up with ice, hardening inside my skin, like glass IV tubes I could never pull out and never shatter, and I made a vow I would never be played by anyone again.

THE TRUTH ABOUT ELLIE

ON TUESDAY, I PAID A VISIT TO JANE THOMAS. AS EDITOR, SHE was leading the staff meeting and doling out assignments. I requested a private conference, and when she shot me an irritated look, sweeping her hand in the direction of her reporters, I said, "I'm here to finish what Maria Salvador started."

That got her attention. Jane yanked me into a corner and I nearly tripped over my feet.

"You have proof teachers have been tampering with grades?" she whispered.

"No. I used to have proof, but not anymore. I have something else that could help vindicate Maria. I have proof an LSD assembly lab is operating at night, right here in the school. I have dates and times. But it's going to cost you."

"I told you, I never pay for stories," said Jane.

"All I want in return is a printout of Ellie Chen's file. I want to see where she sent her transcripts, see where she applied."

"You were awfully cuddly at Café Kismet yesterday. Everyone knows you're back together. Why don't you just ask her where she's going?" Jane wondered.

"I *have* asked her. Her answers don't add up. If I can see for myself, then I'll rest easy."

"Pretend I agree, and I hand over her file," said Jane. "What if you don't like what you find out? Will you take it out on the messenger?"

"I won't."

"You really have proof of this alleged drug lab?" she said.

"Photos."

At the mall with Ellie the previous night, I'd picked up a key-chain camera, the kind Salvador had used, and I'd brought it with me to school. I was in possession of photos of Ryder (from the neck down), the chem lab, and the supplies.

Maybe it wouldn't stop him. Maybe it was useless information. But at least he couldn't use school anymore. At least I could put a stop to that.

I handed over the key chain. I hadn't made any backups; I was beyond that now. Beyond caring, beyond planning ahead with foolproof ideas in the hopes of finding justice or peace. There was no justice for Maria Salvador. There was no peace for her or her family.

Jane told me to come back at the end of fifth and she'd give me an answer.

I did as requested, and still she held out on me.

"Just ask yourself, wouldn't you rather talk to Ellie about this instead of going behind her back?"

"I want to know if I can trust her."

"I think the real question is, can she trust you?" Jane pointed out.

"If you're using the material I gave you, hand over Ellie's file. If you're not using the material, we can forget the whole thing."

She pursed her lips, then handed me the file.

I didn't wait to get home to open it. I found a vacant desk in the journalism room and tore through it. Transcripts and jewelry portfolios had been e-mailed out, all right. Plenty of them. The closest place she'd applied was Northwestern. There were even transcripts sent to England and Ireland. Three or four to New York. And of course the acceptance from Maine.

There was no transcript sent to Lambert College.

The bell rang, a droning sound I was pretty sure I'd hear the rest of my life.

I invited Ellie over that night and we sat in the backyard under the awning, even though it was windy and dark. The San Gabriel Mountains loomed overhead, the impenetrable fortress between Palm Valley and the rest of the world, perpetually keeping us out.

"I don't know why I'm surprised," I said. "You were always going to leave, from the moment you moved here. It was your main attribute."

"What are you talking about, Charlie?" she asked, puzzled. She rested her slim fingers on my arm. "I'm not going anywhere."

"Not yet, but you will be. In the fall."

"Not this again," she said, drawing her hand back and clenching it in her lap. "I know it freaked you out seeing all those brochures. And I'll admit, my dad wants me to go someplace else. But I don't care! I can go to Lambert! Okay? This is the last time we're going to have this conversation. I mean it."

"Stop lying," I said. "Stop lying!"

She jumped at my voice, looking scared. "I'm not lying. Why won't you just believe me?"

I felt like a scab she'd picked off and discarded, leaving behind a small, pinched scar. "Face it, it was never going to last between us. Not the first time, and definitely not this time. I was never your long-haul boyfriend. I was just your California boyfriend, the one you look back on fondly, on the way to better things."

"Or not so fondly," Ellie snapped. She was done being scared of me and had moved on to being angry. "I'm not sure what I'm being accused of here?"

But I barely heard her. I'd started a good circular ramble, and I wasn't ready to take the off ramp. "Your California boyfriend who always pays for gas and soda and movie tickets—that is, when you deign to go to the movies, that lower-class pursuit, God forbid—the easygoing boyfriend, quick to make you laugh, buy you presents, eager to please, do whatever you want, even if it's never what *I* want. I don't think you ever really knew me, and now you're leaving me behind but you refuse to admit it! Just admit it."

Ellie stared at me. Tears fell from her eyes and dripped onto the table. It made me think of Jonathan, at the top of the stairs, the flash drive in his hand.

So there it was; I'd said it. She didn't know me. I didn't even know myself.

There were no correct answers to the multiple-choice questions of me. That's why my parents could never quite figure me out, pin me down. There was only Ellie with a pencil, filling in the dots and then changing her mind, erasing them, and seeing what formed up in their place; altering people's futures, like Donovan and his tests.

The only thing I knew about myself was that I was drunk again, and by my incoherent monologue, Ellie knew it, too. I'd taken a hit of vodka before she arrived; Granddad's latest drink of choice.

"I would've become whoever it was that would make you stay. But now I know it doesn't matter," I said, standing up and swaying on my feet. "And it never did. But it's okay, Ellie. I get it," I added bitterly. "You're doing what you have to do. At MECA. In Maine."

"I still don't understand what you're saying. If I get accepted at Lambert, I'll go there," Ellie said, remaining at the table, staring up at me with tear-glossed eyes.

"It's pretty difficult to be accepted at a college you never applied to, don't you think?"

"I'm telling you, I applied," she sobbed.

"And I'm telling you *I know you're lying*. I'm so sick of guessing what you might like. I'm so sick of worrying about when you're going to leave me. And now that I know, I just want you to admit it." I got down on my knees and clasped my hands together. I really did. "Please, Ellie, just admit it."

She closed her eyes, rubbed the tears off her cheeks. It was a long time before she spoke. "Sex was a big deal to me," she said at last.

I think she was thinking of the safety bar, my arm across her chest. The feeling that told her the ride was just beginning; it was only going to get better and more exciting, but I'd be with her the whole way, dependable and safe.

"If I didn't think we had a future, I wouldn't have had sex with you," she finished.

I stood up and dusted off my knees. "It was a big deal to me, too," I said, but I might've been lying. I might've wanted it to be true, or felt that it should've been true, but the sex was always secondary. The sex was a side effect of being together; it hadn't bound us any closer. It hadn't made the relationship any more likely to succeed; it hadn't kept her with me. "Just tell me the truth. You're not going to college with me, and you never were."

She cried into her hands, and I watched her back rise and fall, her delicate shoulder blades shivering. When she stopped, a minute or so later, her eyes were pink and her face looked puffy.

She approached me, and I looked away: at the ground, at our shoes, anyplace but at her eyes.

"I really did love you," she said. "I'm sorry you don't believe me. I'm sorry you don't trust me. I'm sorry you think I don't know you." Her voice was distorted, magnified by her tears. "I didn't realize you were so angry at me. Good-bye, Charlie. Please don't talk to me at school."

She weaved, a dizzy mess, and when she reached the end of the yard, she tripped, and fell into the grass.

I didn't help her up.

I walked inside and picked up Granddad's left-behind bottle of vodka and poured myself another slosh with trembling hands.

A minute later, the garage opened. I downed my drink and filled part of the vodka bottle with tap water to replace what I'd taken. You water it down enough times and sooner or later the only person it affects is you. If I changed the cells out one by one, at what point did it stop being liquor and start being water, the drink I'd truly wanted all along?

Dad walked in and saw me standing by the sink. I pretended to be filling my glass with water.

"Did I see Ellie outside? She looked terrible."

"Yeah, she just left. Things . . . It didn't work out. Between us."

"But you guys seemed so close on Saturday . . . and with her going to Lambert next year . . . I thought you had a good shot."

"She's not going to Lambert. She never sent in her paperwork. She told me she had, but she hadn't."

"No, I saw her Friday morning. She dropped off her portfolio in person. I saw her outside the admissions office and we said hello."

The glass I was holding fell to the floor, where it clattered and rolled away, but it also stayed with me, waiting to be filled.

It was inside me, in the place where my happiness was supposed to be.

SPRING BREAK

THE MONEY WAS MINE TO SPEND, SO I GAVE MY COLLEGE fund, every last dollar, to Maria Salvador's family. I couldn't go to Lambert College now even if I'd wanted to.

"Is this because of Ellie?" my parents wanted to know.

"It's not because of Ellie," I said, explaining *myself* for once, so they wouldn't have to. I knew myself better now, like an acquaintance I was still getting used to, more and more each day. "It's because of me, of how I lived. So long as the ref doesn't see, it's okay; so long as you don't get caught, you can do whatever you want. I feel like I have to do this—I have to help her. Even if that means working for a year or two and saving up and starting over. Maybe what happened to Maria wasn't my fault. Maybe it was the fault of too many people to name, and I was just one of them."

"Maybe I was one of them, too," said Mom, and when she went to brush my hair off my forehead, I let her.

I told them the whole story, from the drunken party, to my quest to find the flash drive, to the flash drive's contents, to Ryder's betrayal and my own foolishness.

They had no theories about me now. I was impossible to

understand, like a Chekhov story, minus the Russian or the literary quality or an ending. I'd just have to find a way to continue from this point, start a new chapter, and hurtle toward whatever it was I was going to become.

I'd finally stumped my parents, so they listened until I was through.

For the next two months I visited Salvador once a week after school, hoping upon hope she'd wake up, the way I was trying to.

On the first day of spring break, I walked out of the hospital and Ellie was there, standing by my car. We hadn't spoken since the day she'd staggered away from me in my backyard.

"So where exactly has Amelia traveled? Where's the farthest she's ever been?" Ellie asked.

I set my backpack in the car and turned to face her. "Besides California? Nowhere."

"Don't you think it's time she went someplace? Got a real voyage under her belt?"

"I didn't name her after Amelia Earhart," I said bluntly, shoving my hands in my pockets. "I named her after Amelia Pond. She's a character on *Doctor Who*. I didn't want you to know, so I pretended it was something else. I didn't want you to think I was a sci-fi nerd who watched too much TV."

Ellie looked down, shoulders sagging, regret etched across her face. "I hate that I came across so judgmental, that you felt you couldn't tell me things."

"I wish I had been real with you," I said.

We sat with this information a while, rolling it around in our heads and knocking it away like we were working triggers on a pinball machine. The outcome was always the same, though; the thought always came back, always fell down the slot:

GAME OVER

I'd never believed Ellie could be with me long-term, so in the end, I made it true. I'd been wrong about Ryder, so I needed to be right about her. Pushing her away was the only way I got to be right.

It still hurt to think about Ryder. Although he was unidentifiable in the key chain photos, after the images ran in the *Palm Valley High Recorder,* he dropped out of school. I heard he was lying low for a while at the Mobile Estates by himself while his mom finished rehab. I liked to think he spent his days playing MLB on Griffin's Xbox.

Strangely enough, I never pictured him in the chem lab, arranging bundles of drugs for distribution. I still associated him with Little League, but in my mind's eye I didn't watch him throw the bat anymore. I watched everyone else.

I watched the people in the stands, waiting for Ryder to run around the bases, waiting for a moment that was never going to happen. Nobody thought to look at the baseball he'd hit, soaring up through the sky, leaving all of us behind. Nobody thought to see how far it went, or whether it would ever come down. Someone should've looked.

I should've looked.

With Ryder out of the way, I'd been an undisputed soccer star. For a while, anyway. So I didn't look too closely at the situation; I didn't try too hard to find out why he'd failed his drug test, I just accepted it as his choice and my good fortune.

And when he came to me about making extra cash by leaving the history window unlocked, I didn't look too closely then, either. I should've opened my eyes—not so I could avoid the pitfalls of being Ryder's friend, but so I could've helped him. Instead, I gathered all my suspicions together and put them on Ellie. I chose the wrong person to watch, and then I didn't see either of them for who they really were.

"Where did Amelia Pond travel?" Ellie asked.

"Well, they have a time machine called a TARDIS, so pretty much anywhere in space and time."

"Did she ever go to New Mexico?"

"You know, I think she went to the desert once, but never New Mexico." We leaned against my car for a moment, watching the other cars in the parking lot come and go.

"Blue-razz?" Ellie asked, holding out a lollipop. I declined.

"Do you remember what you said about my arm being like a safety bar on a roller coaster?" I asked.

She nodded.

"I think it was holding you back, it was keeping you from escaping. And I'm sorry about that," I said.

She swallowed. "I didn't want to escape. It was my fault, too. For what happened. I gave you a lot of mixed signals because I didn't know what I wanted. But it wasn't because I didn't care about you. You were the only guy I wanted to be with."

"If it helps, knowing what I wanted didn't help me. It didn't make things any easier. It just made me scared all the time of losing what I had, of being forced to live a reality-based life." I looked away for a moment, then met her eyes again. She gazed back without reservation.

"Will you and Amelia drive me to New Mexico? Show me your old stomping grounds and help me check out a college there? We can stop anyplace you're interested, too, on the way, or back."

I looked over at her in surprise. The sun was behind her, framing her face in a kind of harsh halo. In California the last thing you need is more sunshine. Things die from too much sun just as surely as they die without it. A cloud was what I wanted. A cloud was what I needed. A downpour. New Mexico had those sometimes in the spring when the snow melted, and I was overdue.

We drove to my house so I could ask my parents.

I didn't let myself dwell on the what-ifs. I didn't ask myself what it meant, whether Ellie and I could be friends or whether we'd even see each other again after this road trip. Because it didn't matter. I didn't think we'd get back together, but for the next few days, I could finally introduce her to the real me.

I didn't wonder how she'd react to things I did or said, I didn't second-guess my every breath, I just breathed.

When we exited onto the 14 Freeway, headed out of Palm Valley,

I took stock of my senses: the sound of the other cars around us, the heavy breeze on my arm as I dangled it out the window.

The light was so bright it burned my eyes, but I didn't look away. That was the price of keeping them open.

ACKNOWLEDGMENTS

THANKS TO MY AGENT, SARA MEGIBOW, FOR SUPPORTING
me both professionally and personally. Your enthusiasm, kindness,
and publishing knowledge are cherished.

Big thanks to the talented Maggie Lehrman, who helped me
get this story just right. I can't fathom a better editor for *High and
Dry*. You rock!

Thank you to everyone at the Nelson Lit Agency for their hard
work: Kristin Nelson, Anita Mumm, Angie Hodapp, Becky Taylor,
and Lori Bennett.

Amulet Books is a tremendous place to be published. I'm proud
and grateful to be part of the team. Thanks to Susan Van Metre,
Laura Mihalick, Erica La Sala, Jason Wells, Maria T. Middleton, and
Jim Armstrong. ALA Midwinter in January 2013 was a highlight for
me. Next up: Vegas!

Thanks to the Hoovers, Skiltons, and Murphys for your love and
encouragement.

Big thanks to my critique partners and fellow writers Sarvenaz
Tash, Amy Spalding, Kristen Kittscher, and Miranda Kenneally.
Thanks to the generous Hope Larson for hosting Writing Nights,
where all of my brainstorming and much of my writing got done
during a chaotic year.

Thanks to Stephanie Sagheb for Movie Nights! Also, Robyn

Sommerfield, Lisa Gail Green, Julie Musil, Leslie Rose, Cat Winters, Elisabeth Dahl, Den Shewman, Juleen Woods, Stan Zalesny, and Shona and Miya have been wonderfully supportive and I'm very happy to know you all.

At Breakdown Services, Gary, Kathleen, Richard, Kathy, Lynne, and Irene have supported my efforts all the way and kept me laughing during very busy days. Thank you!

Thanks to the fabulous YA and children's mystery writers at Sleuths, Spies and Alibis, as well as the Lucky 13s debut author group.

The works of Rob Thomas, Rian Johnson, Dashiell Hammett, Raymond Chandler, Mercedes Lambert, and Dorothy B. Hughes helped inspire this book.

Lastly, thank you to Joe for sharing your thoughts on my boy narrator and other aspects of writing. You're the best husband, partner, and father to our son I could wish for.

ABOUT THE AUTHOR

SARAH SKILTON is the author of *Bruised*, which received a starred review from *Publishers Weekly* and which *The Horn Book* called "nuanced and honest." She lives with her magician husband and their son in Los Angeles, California.

This book was designed by Jessie Gang and art directed by Maria T. Middleton. The text is set in 9.5-point The Serif Light, a typeface designed by the Dutch typographer Lucas de Groot in 1994 as part of the extensive Thesis font family. The display type is Jersey M54.

This book was printed and bound by R. R. Donnelley in Crawfordsville, Indiana. Its production was overseen by Elizabeth Peskin.